FACE
TO
FACE

Treutlen County Library
PO Box 49
Soperton, GA 30457
(912) 529-6683

G·K
Hall
&C?

Also by Ellery Queen
in Large Print:

There Was an Old Woman
The Finishing Stroke
The Dutch Shoe Mystery
And Then on the Eighth Day
Ten Days Wonder

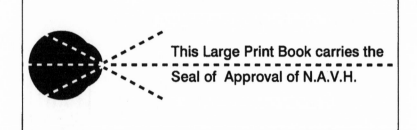

This Large Print Book carries the
Seal of Approval of N.A.V.H.

FACE
TO
FACE

Ellery Queen

G.K. Hall & Co. • Thorndike, Maine

Copyright © 1967 by Ellery Queen
Copyright renewed.

All rights reserved.

Published in 2000 by arrangement with Frederic Dannay and Manfred B. Lee Literary Property Trusts and their agent, JackTime, 3 Erold Court, Allendale, NJ 07401.

G.K. Hall Large Print Paperback Series.

The text of this Large Print edition is unabridged.
Other aspects of the book may vary from the original edition.

Set in 16 pt. Plantin by Rick Gundberg.

Printed in the United States on permanent paper.

Library of Congress Cataloging-in-Publication Data

Queen, Ellery.
   Face to face / by Ellery Queen.
    p. cm.
   ISBN 0-7838-9037-0 (lg. print : sc : alk. paper)
   1. Large type books. I. Title.
  PS3533.U4 F33 2000
  813'.52—dc21   00-029569

CONTENTS

1 PROFILE

There is in every human countenance either a history or a prophecy.

S. T. COLERIDGE

ONE

On the penultimate lap of his round-the-planet tour, pumping police chiefs in odd cities for usable stories, Ellery had planned an overnight stop in London. But on flying in from Orly he ran into an Interpol man in Commissioner Vail's office at New Scotland Yard. The Interpol man was *muy simpático,* one good yarn led to another in a procession of pubs, and before he knew it several days and nights had blinked by, putting the New Year just around the corner.

The next morning, spurred by conscience and a head, Emery stopped in at the airline office to pick up his ticket. And that was how and when he met Harry Burke. Burke was negotiating passage on the same jet to New York.

The Interpol man introduced Burke as a private inquiry agent — "one of the best, Queen, which of course means he doesn't pad his expense account by more than ten percent." Burke laughed; he was a short sandy-haired man with the neck of a wrestler who looked like a good companion for a fight. He had very light, almost transparent, eyes and they had a trick of disappearing, as if they were not there at all. He looked like a Teuton, the "Burke" said he should have talked with a brogue, but his speech came out on the burry side, and before leaving them together Interpol cheerfully identified him as a renegade Scot.

Over a pint and a much sucked-on pipe in the nearest pub, Burke said: "So you're Queen the Younger. This is fantastic."

"It is?" Emery said.

"Meeting you this way, I mean. I was with your father not fifteen hours ago."

"*My* father?"

"Inspector Richard Queen of the New York police department," Burke said solemnly.

"You've just flown in?"

The Scot nodded.

"But I saw you buy a plane ticket back to New York a few minutes ago."

"I found a cable from Inspector Queen waiting for me when I got off the plane. Seems there's been a development in the case that originally took me to the States. He wants me to turn right around and fly back."

"That's my daddy," said Ellery. "Does he mention why?"

"No, but the cable contains that salty word, 'pronto.' "

"It must be important." Ellery fondly accepted another ale from the barmaid, who looked as if she could have fetched the entire keg on one palm. "This case, Burke. Could it be the sort of thing I have no strength to resist?"

"I don't know your capacity for punishment."

Burke smiled at the vast barmaid, too, and buried his Caledonian nose in the mug. He was a handsome man.

They made the westward crossing shoulder to shoulder. For all the good Ellery's hinting did, the Scotsman might have been from the CIA. On subjects unrelated to his case, however, he was talkative enough. Harry Burke was an ex-Yard man who had recently resigned his detective inspectorship to form an agency of his own. Business was picking up, he said wryly.

"In the beginning it was touch and go. If not for my connections at the Yard, I'd be scratching like a Bantu. Commissioner Vail has been very kind." Ellery gathered that Burke's current professional preoccupation was a result of Vail's latest kindness. The inquiry had come into the Yard and the Commissioner, finding it not proper Yard business, had privately recommended Burke for the job. It was not, Ellery suspected, Vail's first kindness of the sort. Burke was kept hopping now.

"But I'm a bachelor," the sandy-haired man said, "and I don't have to make a ruddy accounting to some whining female for my hours. No, there's no one on the agenda, thank you. I don't stay in one place long enough to form an attachment."

"You," quoth Ellery, speaking strictly from hearsay, "are the sort who gets hooked in one fell jerk."

"The angler hasn't been born who can hook me."

11

"Watch out for the ones on my side of the puddle. Catching the hard ones comes naturally to American women."

"They seem to have missed you, Queen."

"Oh, but I'm the original Artful Dodger."

"Then we have a great deal in common."

And so they proved to have, including a penchant for small disagreements. By the time they set down in Gander they were on a first-name basis and arguing amiably over the comparative merits of serving Scotch kippers with and without sautéed onions. They almost forgot to mark the passage of the old year, which took place between heaven and earth after the flight resumed.

They landed at Kennedy International Airport early New Year's morning in a fog only slightly less gothic than the one that had grounded them in Gander.

"There's no point in your groping about for a hotel room at this hour," Ellery said. "Come on home with me, Harry."

"Oh, no. I couldn't put you and the Inspector out."

"Rubbish, there's a daybed in my study. Besides, it will give you a jump on whatever my father's brought you back to New York for." But this delicate feeler brought forth from Harry Burke no more than a good-natured nod. "Taxi?"

Their cab drove uptown through Times Square, which looked like a ghost town invaded by tumbleweed. "People are a mucky lot, aren't they?" Burke remarked, pointing his pipe stem at the litter. "Every time I see a thing like this I think of that last scene in *On the Beach.*"

"Maybe that's what they were thinking of, too."

They achieved the Queen apartment and found the Inspector not in his bed, or anywhere. "Out celebrating?" Burke ventured.

"Not a chance. Not my daddy. It's a case. What's this?"

This was a message for Ellery propped against the typewriter in his study, inscribed in the old man's squibby hand.

Dear Son:
A Miss Roberta West of East 73rd St. wants you to call her. No matter what time you get in, she says. Me, I'm up to my ears in something. I'll be phoning you. Oh, yes. Happy New Year!

It was signed "Dad" and there was a telephone number.

"Is this a sample of the Queens' home life?" asked the Scotsman.

"Only when interrupted by mayhem. Dad and I usually spend New Year's Eve dozing at the telly." Ellery dialed the number. "Dump your bags in my bedroom, Harry — it's in there. Oh, and there's a bar in the living room if you'd like an eye-opener. Hello?"

"Ellery Queen?" asked a deeply anxious voice.

"Yes. I have a message to call a Miss West."

"I'm Miss West. It's wonderful of you to call

me so early. Whoever answered said you were flying in from England. Did you just get in, Mr. Queen?"

"Just. What's this about, Miss West?"

"Are you calling from your home?"

"Yes?"

"I'd like to come over."

"Now?" asked Ellery astonished. "I need a shave, I haven't had breakfast, and sleeping on transatlantic planes isn't one of my accomplishments. Can't this wait?"

"I haven't slept, either, waiting for your call. Please?"

She sounded like a pretty girl. So he sighed and said, "Do you know the address?"

TWO

Roberta West proved even prettier than she sounded. The moment Ellery set eyes on her he labeled her "theater," with "little?" in parentheses. She was dainty of body and fair of skin, with true sorrel hair, luminous eyes that were underscored with late hours or trouble, and an enchanting birthmark on her upper right cheek that looked remarkably like a little butterfly. Ellery's dramatic deduction derived from a number of small observations — the way she walked and cocked her head, a certain tension in her posture, an impression of newly acquired muscle-discipline, and above all the studied diction, as if even its slight occasional slurring had been carefully rehearsed. She was dressed in skirt and sweater-blouse of some angoralike material, with a Parisian-looking coat flung over her shoulders, a scarf wound about her neck that might have been designed by Picasso, and gauntlet gloves. Her tiny feet were expensively shod in stylish flats, with butterfly bows — a touch, Ellery noted, that balanced the birthmark on her cheek; he was sure the bows had been chosen for just that reason.

The whole woman was an artful study in casualness — so much so, in fact, that Ellery was tempted to doubt his own conclusions. When they looked as if they had just stepped out of the pages of *Vogue*, he had found, they were almost always somebody's office help.

"You're in the theater," he said.

Her brilliant, nearly fevered, eyes widened. "How did you know, Mr. Queen?"

"I have my methods," he grinned, seeing her into the living room. "Oh, this is Mr. Burke. Miss West."

The girl murmured something, and Harry Burke said, "D'ye do," in a startled way, as if he had just stumbled over something. He moved over toward the doorway to Ellery's study and said with plain reluctance, "I'll wash up, Ellery. Or something."

"Maybe Miss West won't mind your sitting in on this," Ellery said. "Mr. Burke is a private detective, in from London on business."

"Oh, in that case," the girl said quickly; and for some reason she lowered her head. As for Burke, his glance at Ellery was positively canine. He slithered over to one of the windows and stood there, out of the way, staring.

"Now," Ellery said when he had the girl seated, had offered her breakfast and been refused, and lit a cigaret for her, "shall we get down to cases, Miss West?"

She was quiet for a moment. Then she said, "I hardly know where to start," looking confused; but suddenly she leaned over and rapped her

16

cigaret ash into a tray. "I suppose you remember Glory Guild?"

Ellery remembered Glory Guild. He would have had to be deficient in all senses to profess amnesia. He not only remembered Glory Guild, he had listened to her with both enraptured ears in his youth, he had had wishful dreams about her — an international trauma — and even the memory of her voice sufficed to tickle his giblets. Memories were all that were left to those whom the press agent in her heyday had, with unfortunate failure to refer to the dictionary, termed her "myrmidons" of admirers.

Oh, yes, he had heard of GeeGee, as her intimates were said to call her (he had never been one of them, alas, alas); he still occasionally spun one of her old 78s on a moonlit night when he was feeling his years. He was surprised to have her name thrust at him so abruptly. It was as if the girl with the sorrel hair had recalled Helen Morgan, or Galli-Curci, or the little girl with the palpitant throat in *The Wizard of Oz*.

"What about Glory Guild?" Ellery asked. A movement by Harry Burke, swiftly stilled, had told him that Burke was surprised, too; surprised, and something more. Ellery slavered to know what it was. But then he compelled his attention to revert to Roberta West.

"I'm in love with Glory Guild's husband," the girl said and the way she said it brought Ellery to the point. "I mean, I ought to say I *was* in love with Carlos." It seemed to Ellery that she shud-

17

dered, something he had found very few people did in actuality, regardless of authors. Then she said, "How can women be such fools? Such blind fools?" She really said "blind fools."

She began to cry.

Crying women were no novelty in the Queen living room, and the obvious cause of these tears was one of the commonest; still, Ellery was touched, and he let her cry it quite out. She stopped at last, sniffing like a child, groped in her bag for a handkerchief, and pawed at her little nose. "I'm sorry," the girl said. "I hadn't meant to do that. I'd made up my mind I *wouldn't*. Anyway, it was all over seven months ago. Or I thought it was. But now something's happened . . ."

THREE

Roberta West's story came out episodic and random, a mosaic tumbled to fragments that had to be put together by the bit. As Ellery reconstructed it, it began with a sketch of Glory Guild, her life and works.

She had been born Gloria Guldenstern in 1914, in Sinclair Lewis country; and in the 30s she had come out of the Midwest with Lewisite fidelity to take New York by storm and, inevitably, the wide country. She had never had a music lesson in her life; she was completely self-taught — voice, musicology, piano. She played her own accompaniments.

It was said of Glory Guild that she also played her voice. Certainly her singing technique was as calculated as the notes on her music paper. There was a throb of passion, almost of grief, in her projection that swayed audiences like the fakir's reed — faint and faraway, something not quite lost. In nightclubs it silenced even drunks. The critics called it an *intime* voice, fit for bistros; and yet, so pervasive was her magic, it affected multitudes. By the end of the 30s she was singing weekly on her own radio show to tens of millions of listeners. She was America's radio darling.

She came on the air to the strains of "Battle Hymn of the Republic," a signature played sweet and slow by her 42-piece orchestra; in the nature of things in those simpler days, a columnist nicknamed her Glory-Glory. Glory-Glory was otherwise a shrewd, practical woman. Her smartest act was to place her fortunes in the stringy hands of Selma Pilter, the theatrical agent, who quickly became her business manager as well as booker. Mrs. Pilter (there had been a Mr. Pilter, but he had vanished in the mists of some antique divorce court) managed Glory's affairs so astutely that, at the time of her loss of voice and retirement in 1949, the singer was said to be a millionaire.

In her limited way Glory had a questing mind; retirement threw her back not merely upon music but on puzzles, her other passion. She was a hifi fanatic long before the pursuit of the perfect tweeter became a national aberration; her library of contemporary music was a collector's dream. The motivation for her absorption in puzzles was less clear. She had come from a rural Minnesota family whose interest in such pastimes had never risen above the ancient copy of Sam Lloyd in the farmhouse parlor. Nevertheless, Glory spent many hours with crosswords, Double-Crostics, anagrams, and detective stories (the classic bafflers of the field — she had no use for the sex-and-violence or psychological mysteries that began to clog the paperback racks after World War II). Both her New York apartment and her hideaway cottage — nestled in a stand of packed pines on a lakefront near Newtown, Connecticut — were cluttered with players, discs, FM radios, electronic recording equipment (she could not bear to part with it), musical instruments, mountains of mystery stories and puzzle books and gadgets; and on her own open terrace such gimmickry as a set of *buinho* chairs, handwoven in Portugal of wet reeds, whose marvelous secret was that each time they were rained on their weave tightened.

Glory had remained single during her singing career, although she was a deep-breasted, handsome blonde much (if gingerly) pursued. When her voice went back on her at the age of 35, the senseless trick of fate sent her into Garbo-like seclusion, and (as in Garbo's case) it was assumed, in the media where such speculations are of earth-shaking concern, that she would never marry. And she did hold out for nine years. But then in 1958, when she was 44 and he was 33, she met Count Carlos Armando. Within three months they were man and wife.

The "Count" Armando was a self-conferred title which no one, least of all Carlos, took seriously. His origin had a floating base; not even his name could be taken for granted. He was altogether charming about it. He claimed Spanish, Roman, Portuguese, and mixed Greek-and-Romanian descent as the fancy took him; once he even said his mother had been an Egyptian. One of his friends of the international set (a real count) laughed, "In direct descent from Cleopatra, obviously," and Carlos, showing his brilliant teeth, laughed back, "Of course, *caro*. By way of Romeo." Those who claimed the worthiest information asserted that his parents had been gypsies and that he had been born in a caravan by the side of some squalid Albanian road. It might well have been so.

None of this seemed to make any difference to the women in his life. Like obedient tin soldiers, they fell to his amorous fire in ranks. He kept his ammunition dry as a matter of working principle, careful not to allow it to sputter away because of an honest emotion. Women were his profession. He had never worked an otherwise gainful day in his life.

Carlos's first marriage, when he was 19, had been to an oil dowager from Oklahoma. She was exactly three times his age, with a greed for male youth that amused him. She cast him adrift well within two years, having barged into a beautiful boy from Athens. His severance pay was considerable, and Carlos spent a mad year throwing it away.

His second wife was a wealthy Danish baroness, with the features of a cathedral gargoyle, whose chief delight was to dress his curly black hair as if he were a doll. Four months of lying on couches with those terrible fingers creeping about his head were enough for Carlos; he seduced his wife's bedazzled secretary, contrived to be caught at it, and gallantly insisted on being paid off.

Another year of high life, and Carlos began to look around again.

He discovered a United States senator's juicy little 16-year-old daughter summering in the Alps; the resulting scandal involved a highly paid Swiss abortionist (from whom Carlos collected 15 percent) and a very large senatorial check, conditional upon his silence, with the threat of prosecution to enforce it.

The years marched by, and with them a grand parade of wives, all rich and silly and old enough to be his mother: a New York socialite who divorced her banker husband in order to marry him (this union broke up after a $100,000 brawl at an all-night party in his wife's Newport villa that made tabloid history); an alcoholic Back Bay spinster whose simple escutcheon was first plotted at Plymouth Rock; a Hungarian countess dying of tuberculosis (she left him nothing but a castle surrounded by a stagnant moat and debts — with easy foresight he had run through her fortune before her death); an aging Eurasian ex-beauty he quite literally sold to a rich Turk whose real objective was her nubile daughter (as she had been Carlos's); a Chicago meatpacker's widow who, accompanied by a photographer, surprised him in her maid's bed and booted him out without a penny's salve, even producing the photographs in court to Carlos's smarting surprise — with unsporting disdain for the press.

This debacle left him in financial extremis. He was in great need when he met GeeGee Guild.

Not that Glory was so hard to take; she was still attractive, and younger at their meeting than any of his ex-wives had been. Still, to Carlos the prime question was: Is she rich enough? He had led a cowboy's life herding idleness, and it was beginning to leave its brand on his dark athletic flesh, or so he fancied from increasing self-study in his mirror. The middle-aged and old ones who, like his first wife, sought to lap thirstily from the waterhole of male youth might soon notice the flattening taste of Count Armando. When that day came, the bogus count assured himself glumly, the bellowing kine would turn to greener pasture.

So at this stage of his life, Armando decided, he could not afford to make a mistake. Undercover he made a financial survey of Glory Guild that would not have shamed an ace credit agent. What he found out heartened him, and he stripped down for the conquest.

It was not easy, even though Glory was receptive. She had become lonely and restless, and what she was seeing daily in *her* mirror dismayed her. Between her need for companionship and attention and the hurrying truths revealed by her glass, a young man like Carlos Armando was inevitable. Because she had heard stories about him and glimpsed him for what he was, she hired a reliable agency to check his background. It confirmed what she suspected, and she was determined not to go the way of all the female fools in his life.

"I like having you around," she told Carlos at his proposal of marriage, "and you want my money, or as much of it as you can lay your hands on. Right? Well, I'll marry you on one condition."

"Must we speak of technicalities at a time like this, my darling?" asked Carlos, kissing her hands.

"The condition is this: You will sign a premarital agreement renouncing in advance any share of my estate."

"Ah," said Carlos.

"Even the one-third dower share ordinarily guaranteed by law," said Glory dryly, "the gleam of which I can see in your eye. I've consulted my attorney and, properly drawn up, such a contract would be perfectly legal in this state — I mean in case you have an idea you could break it later."

"What you must think of me, *bonita*," mourned Carlos, "to make such an unfair condition. I am proposing to give you all of myself."

"And quite a hunk it is," said Glory Guild fondly, ruffling his hair (he caught himself in time to keep from flinching.) "So I've worked out what the lawyers call a *quid pro quo*."

"And what is that, my enchantment?" asked Carlos, as if he did not know what a *quid pro quo* was.

"A tit for my tat."

"I see. . . . Time?" Carlos said suddenly. He was intuitive in all matters relating to women.

"That's it, baby. Give me a minimum of five

25

happy years of married life and I'll tear up the contract. I've had you investigated, Carlos, and the longest you've ever stuck to one woman was less than two years. Five are my terms, then zip! goes the contract, and you come into your normal legal rights as my husband."

They looked each other in the eye, and both smiled.

"I love you madly," murmured Carlos, "but love is not all. Agreed."

"Love, shove," said Glory.

And so it was arranged; and he signed the prenuptial agreement, and they were bound in not so holy matrimony.

FOUR

"I met Carlos in Easthampton," continued Roberta West, "while I was doing summer stock. It was at the tail end of the season, and he and Glory came backstage. The director was an old man who made a great to-do over Glory, but she was no more than a name to me — I was a little girl when she retired — and all I could see was an overweight woman with stupidly dyed hair looking like some aging Brünnehilde out of a second-rate opera company and clinging to the arm of a man who seemed young enough to be her son.

"But I thought Carlos was cute, and I suppose I was flattered by the fuss he made over my performance. There's something in Carlos's voice," she added gloomily, "that gets through to women. You know he's a fake, but it doesn't matter. It's not so much what he says as how he says it . . . I suppose I sound like a gullible idiot."

Neither man, being a man, said anything.

"When the stock engagement was over, I hadn't been back in town twenty-four hours — I don't know how he got my phone number, because it was a new one and still wasn't in the book — before he called me. He handed me some transparent story about being awfully impressed by my talent, and how he knew he could pull some strings for me, and wouldn't I like to talk it over? And I fell for it — the oldest line in show business! — knowing all the time that I was letting myself in for trouble. . . . The funny part of it was that he did manage to get me an audition — and the part — in an off-Broadway play. To this day I don't know how, except that the producer was a woman. Men have nothing but contempt for him — or jealousy — but women can't seem to resist his charm. I suppose this producer was one of them, although she's an old bag with a personality like a buzz saw. Anyway, he sweet-talked her into it. The way he did me."

The girl with the sorrel hair half shut her eyes. Then she picked a cigaret out of her bag, and Harry Burke leaped with a lighter. She smiled up at him over the flame, but not as if she saw him.

"He kept turning up . . . Carlos has a persistence that batters you down. No matter how careful you are. . . . I fell in love with him. In a raunchy sort of way he's beautiful. Certainly when he pays attention to a woman she feels that she's the only woman in the world. It becomes total involvement — I don't know — as if you're the absolute center of the universe. And all the time you know he hasn't an honest bone in his body, that he's pulled the same line on hundreds of women. And you don't care. You just *don't* . . . I fell in love with him, and he told me the only thing in the world that would make him happy was to marry me."

28

Ellery stirred. "How well-heeled are you, Miss West?"

She laughed. "I have a small income from a trust, and with what I can earn here and there I just manage to get by. That's what fooled me," said the girl bitterly. "He's never married except for money. Being poor, I began to think that in my case his protestations of love might be, for once in his life, the real thing. How naive can you get! I didn't know what he really had in mind. Until one night, a little more than seven months ago . . ."

For some reason Glory had gone up to her Newtown cottage, and Carlos had seized the opportunity to see Roberta. It was on this occasion that he had finally shown his hand.

Roberta had known about his premarital agreement with his wife, and that the five-year mark had been passed — by that date he and Glory had been married five and a half years. According to Carlos, Glory had torn up their agreement at the expiration of the five years, as she had promised; so that now, if anything were to happen to her, he would inherit at least one-third of her estate under his ordinary dower rights; more, if she had named him in her will, about which he seemed uncertain.

At first, the West girl said, she had not seen what he was driving at. "How could it occur to any normal person? I told him truthfully that I had no idea what he was talking about." Was there something wrong with his wife? Was she incurably ill? Cancer? What?

Carlos had said easily, "She is as healthy as a cow. *Dios!* She will outlive both of us."

"Then do you mean a divorce settlement?" Roberta had asked, confused.

"Settlement? She would not give me a lira if I were to suggest a divorce."

"Carlos, I don't understand."

"Of course you do not, *palomilla mia.* So like a child! But you will listen to me, and I shall tell you how we can be rid of this cow, and marry and enjoy the milk from her udders."

And, calmly, as if he were relating the plot of a novel, Carlos had disclosed his plan to Roberta. Glory stood in the way; she had to be knocked aside. But as her husband he would be the first to be suspected. Unless he had what was called an alibi. But for an alibi to stand up, it had to be unshakable; that is, he, Carlos, truly had to be elsewhere when the thing was done. This was simply arranged, in any of a thousand ways. Who, then, was to do it? Who but she, Roberta, the co-beneficiary of Glory's death? Did she now see?

"I now saw," Roberta told the two silent men. "Oh, how I now saw! In that mocking voice of his, as if he were talking about taking a walk in the park, he was actually proposing that I murder his wife so that he and I could get married and live on the blood money. I was so stunned, so horrified, that for a minute I couldn't get a word out. I guess he took my silence for consent,

30

because he slithered over and tried to make love to me. It broke the spell with a bang. I pushed him away so hard he staggered. This lovely conversation took place in Glory's and Carlos's apartment, and I ran out of there as if the devil were after me. For all I know, he was — he has the devil's own gall. How could I have thought I loved that monster! My skin was crawling. All I could think of was getting away from him. I cabbed home and walked the floor all night, shaking like a leaf."

Carlos had telephoned her the next day, the girl went on, and she had told him never to call or try to see her again and hung up on him.

"The bloody bastard," muttered Harry Burke. He looked as if he could cheerfully have committed murder himself at that moment.

"You were lucky to get out of it without a beating," Ellery commented. "Sometimes these types, when they're balked, can be awfully rough. But, Miss West, I don't get it. If all this happened more than seven months ago — back in May? — why have you waited so long to tell the story? And, in any event, why the urgency now?"

The girl looked puzzled. "The urgency? What do you mean, Mr. Queen? I would have thought —"

"We obviously have our wires crossed," Ellery said with a smile. "There's more to your story?"

"Of course." She glanced from him to Burke. and back again, shaking her head. "Or don't you

31

believe me? I don't understand. As for why I didn't tell anyone all this time — I don't know. It was such a shocking experience, as if I'd dreamed it all. The thought of going to the police, or to someone like you, never entered my mind. For one thing, I kept telling myself he couldn't really have meant it. For another" — her delicate skin colored — "it would have meant getting my relationship with him smeared all over the papers. You know the bit. Anyway, I didn't. And when he didn't call or try to see me again, I put the whole thing out of my head, or tried to. Until it was forcibly recalled to me two nights ago. What's today? Yes, the night before last, Wednesday night."

"The night of December thirtieth?" Harry Burke asked sharply. It made Ellery look at him.

"Yes. Carlos phoned me. I hadn't heard from him, as I said, since late spring. Of course I hung up on him —"

"What did the beggar want?" snapped Burke.

"He had to see me, he said. I told him that what I'd said months ago still went, and banged the receiver. Not a half hour later my apartment bell rang, and when I opened the door, there he was. I tried to shut it in his face, but he stuck his foot in the way. He made such a fuss, in such a loud voice, that I was afraid the neighbors might come running out. So I let him in."

"What *did* he want?" Ellery asked.

"At the time I couldn't imagine. He made no attempt to bring up that fantastic proposition

32

again, just talked about trivial things — me, the plays on Broadway, what he and Glory had been doing recently, and so on. I kept asking him to go, and he kept making conversation. He wasn't drunk, or anything like that — Carlos never drinks enough to lose his head; at least I've never seen him sozzled. I kept getting the feeling he was stalling for time, because he would glance at his watch every once in a while."

"Oh," said Ellery in an odd voice. And "Oh," said Harry Burke, in an even odder voice. But while Ellery's "Oh" had a speculative quality, Burke's was deep with foreboding; and again Ellery wondered.

Roberta West leaned forward in an attitude of tense appeal. "I finally got rid of him at midnight. Or rather at midnight, without warning, he suddenly decided to leave. I remember he looked at his watch again and actually said aloud, 'It's midnight, Roberta, I'll have to go.' As if he had a deadline or something. I didn't understand any of it. Until later. That's really why I'm here, Mr. Queen. He used me!"

"It sounds like it," Ellery agreed. "But for what?"

"Don't you *know?*"

"Don't I know what, Miss West?"

"That Glory Guild Armando was murdered Wednesday night?"

33

FIVE

Ellery had not seen a New York newspaper for a long time, and if GeeGee's murder had been reported in the London *Times*, he had missed the leader in the malty haze of some pub.

As for Harry Burke, the Scot seemed both knowledgeable and appalled. He stalked over to Ellery's bar and poured himself a slug out of the handiest bottle, which happened to be bourbon, and tossed it down neat, with no more awareness of what he was doing than if he had raised his hand to scratch himself.

Ellery kept dividing his attention between the West girl and Burke.

"How dense of me," she was saying. "Of course you don't know about the murder — you've been in Europe. Don't you have this morning's paper?"

"No," Ellery said. "What time did she get it, Miss West, do you know?"

"Not the exact time, no. But I do know, from the news stories, that it was while Carlos was in my apartment Wednesday night. It's perfectly clear now what he was up to. When he couldn't talk me into killing his wife last summer, he started looking around for another patsy. And he must have found her — it has to be a her, Mr. Queen; he wouldn't be able to talk a *man* into giving him the time of day. So Wednesday night, while this woman did the killing — whoever she is — he made it his business to be in my place. Using me as his alibi! Dragging me into this after I thought I was rid of him and his wife and the whole nasty mess!"

She seemed on the edge of hysteria, and Ellery went to some lengths to back her away. Burke was marching like a grenadier before the bar now, evidently struggling with a problem.

"Question," Ellery said to the girl. "Just why have you come to me?"

She was twisting the straps of her bag. "It's that — well, I'm so *alone* in this, Mr. Queen. Up to my neck in a horrible situation through no fault of my own — well, perhaps I *was* at fault to fall for Carlos's line, but how could I have known what I was getting into? Certainly I couldn't have dreamed he was scheming to commit murder. . . . Carlos, of course, must have promptly told the police of his alibi, which meant me, because they've already been to my apartment to question me, and I naturally had to tell them the truth, which is that he was with me Wednesday night until midnight."

"Did you tell the officers about Carlos's proposing to you last May that you murder his wife?"

"No. I guess I should have, but I just couldn't bring myself to. I kept thinking how the more I said, the more deeply I'd get involved. So all I did was answer their questions. What do I do, Mr. Queen? How do I get out of this?"

"I'm afraid it's too late for that. My advice to you is to tell the police everything, and the sooner the better."

She bit her lip.

Ellery said Harry Burke abruptly. "I'd like to talk to you."

"Would you excuse us a moment, Miss West?" When they were in his study, behind the closed door, Ellery said, "You've been bursting with some kind of bombshell since that girl got here, Harry. You're involved in this case, aren't you?"

"I am now," Burke said unhappily. "Until a moment ago I didn't know any more about the murder than you did. But the thing that brought me to New York originally — my first trip here — was tied up with Glory Guild. She'd made a request of the Yard which was outside the Yard's competence, and Vail recommended me to her, as a private agent. It was a routine inquiry — I can't see how it could have anything to do with this, although there's always the possibility." The Scot scowled. "The fact is, Ellery, on Wednesday night I was with the Guild woman in her apartment until a bit after eleven, on the business that brought me overseas. I made my report, and from her place I went directly to the airport. My plane took off a short time later, at 1:00 A.M. I left her alive and well."

"Then she was murdered by someone who got

36

to her place between a few minutes past eleven, when you left her, and midnight, when Armando left Roberta West's apartment."

"It would seem so." Burke seemed troubled about something, but he said nothing more.

Ellery squinted at him. "This matter that brought you to New York — you consulted my father about it?"

"Yes. It required the cooperation of the New York police."

"Then that's why dad cabled you to come back — the hunch that it might have something to do with the killing." Ellery paused, inviting Burke to comment. But Burke did not. "He must have gone on the murder some time after it broke. Apparently when he dashed off this telephone-message note to me he hadn't connected the West girl with the case, or still didn't know any of the facts. These things over here are always handled on the precinct level first. Well, Harry, this puts a different complexion on things. I seem to be in it, too, like it or not."

Burke merely nodded.

They returned to the living room. "All right, Miss West, I'll stick with you," Ellery told the girl. She was staring at them in a frightened way. "At least until we see how it shapes up. The first thing you're going to do is tell the police the whole story. Carlos's alibi notwithstanding, it may well be that he's as guilty of his wife's murder as if he committed it himself. At this point I'd say that it's likelier than not."

37

"I'll do whatever you say, Mr. Queen." She seemed relieved.

"This Armando character is obviously devious. Whoever the woman is he's snake-charmed into doing his dirty work for him, he's probably been seeing her in secret — as he saw you, I take it?"

He could barely hear her "Yes."

"And now he'll be careful not to see her at all, or one of these days he'll pretend he's meeting her for the first time. He's got to wait for the heat to let up. Well, we'll see. She may be his weakness, too. At any rate, she has to be found, and I have the feeling it won't be easy."

Just then the phone rang in Ellery's study.

"Son?" It was his father's nasal rasp. "So your plane finally landed, did it? What did it do, play skipping stones all the way from London? Ellery, I'm on one beaut of a case —"

"I know," said Ellery. "Glory, Glory Hallelujah."

"So the West girl did get to you. She was questioned by some precinct men, and I didn't put two and two together till after I got the early reports. Is she there now?"

"Yes."

"Well, come on over and join the party, and bring her with you. By the way, you didn't happen to run into a man named Harry Burke on the plane coming over, did you?"

"I did. And he's with me. House guest."

"I'll be damned," said the Inspector. "Another of your magic acts. I've been waiting to hear from Burke — I suppose he's told you I cabled him. Bring him along, too."

"Where are you, dad?"

"At GeeGee's Park Avenue apartment. Do you know the address?"

"No, but Burke and Miss West do."

"That's a fact, isn't it?" The old man cursed and hung up.

SIX

The doorman at the cooperative had a wild look in his eye. There was a patrolman conspicuously on duty in the lobby, and another in the foyer of the Guild-Armando apartment. Several detectives, including Sergeant Velie, were working their way through the penthouse duplex. Ellery left Roberta West in a small drawing room off the foyer, and at Velie's direction he and Harry Burke went up the wrought-iron stairway to the master bedroom, where they found Inspector Queen going through a clothes closet.

"Oh, hello, son," the old man said, barely looking up. "Damn it, where *is* it? Sorry to bring you all the way back across an ocean, Burke, but I had no choice. It's got to be here *somewhere*."

"Before we get down to cases, daddy-o," Ellery said in a pained tone, "may I point out that you haven't seen me for almost two months? I didn't expect the fatted calf, but could you spare a handshake?"

"Oh . . . *booshwa*," said the Inspector crossly, falling back on the slang of his youth. "Help me find it, you two, will you?"

"Find what, Inspector?" asked Burke. "What are you looking for?"

40

"Her diaries. I'm mad for cases where they keep diaries. Her secretary, Jeanne Temple, tells me Glory-Glory kept one ever since her retirement — wrote up the events of the day every night before going to bed. By now it's volumes. A few months ago she started working on a publishing project, an autobiography or book of memoirs or something, with the help of that gigolo husband of hers and Miss Temple, and she's been using the diaries as reference material, where she couldn't trust her memory or had to look up details. And that's great, only where are they? Or it? I'm anxious to see the latest one especially, the current diary — what she wrote in it Wednesday night. If she did, that is. We've been searching for two days."

"They're all missing?" asked Ellery.

"Including the manuscript of the autobiography."

"Inspector," said Harry Burke. "I saw her Wednesday night."

"The hell you did. I was hoping for a break like that! It's one of the reasons I cabled you. What time was it you left her?"

"A few minutes after eleven."

"That's good, that's good," the Inspector said in an absent way. "She wasn't excited or nervous or anything?"

"Not as far as I could tell. Of course I didn't know her very well — just the few conversations we'd had about the matter I was on for her."

"Well, those diaries are tied into this case

41

some way, I'll bet a cookie, or the whole kit and caboodle wouldn't be missing. They've been lifted. The question is, why?"

Ellery was looking over the Hollywood bed, with its bold satin spread and silken bolsters and gold damask draped canopy. The bed had not been slept in.

His father caught the glance and nodded. "She never did get to bed Wednesday night."

"I take it, dad, she wasn't killed in this room."

"No." The Inspector led the way past a vast master bath with a sunken marble tub and gold-plated fixtures, into an untidy den — if it had been human, Ellery would have called it disheveled. "She was shot in here."

Except for the clutter, the room was surprisingly Spartan. One scatter rug on the parquet floor, a kneehole desk and a leather swivel chair behind it, facing the doorway; a far-out armchair of some black wood, covered with what Ellery could have sworn was elephant hide; one work of art on a pedestal, a carving in ebony of a Watusi warrior, of native African craftsmanship, and not very good, he thought. There was not a painting on the wall, and the lamp beside the armchair had a mica shade that was flaking. High above the Watusi warrior, inset in the wall near the ceiling, was a wood-framed grille of some coarse, potato-sacklike material, with a volume regulator, which Ellery took to conceal a speaker that piped music in from the elaborate player he had noticed in the living room downstairs; he had seen a similar speaker in one of the bedroom walls, and one in the bathroom. And that was all except for the bookcases, which ran around three walls to a height of some eight feet. The shelves were mobbed with books — lying down, leaning both ways, protruding (chiefly detective stories, Ellery noted with interest — he spotted Poe, Gaboriau, Anna Katharine Green, Wilkie Collins, Doyle, Freeman, Christie, Sayers, Van Dine among many others, including a number of his own early books); scrapbooks of all sizes and colors, tricks, puzzles, whatnots . . . the accumulation of what must have been many years. Ellery strolled over to one shelf and plucked a Double-Crostics book at random from a small army of them. He riffled through it; all the puzzles had been completed, in ink. In his experience, there was nothing quite so useless as a filled-in Double-Crostics book, especially one filled in in ink, the mark of the thirty-third degree. Glory Guild Armando had evidently been unable to part with anything relating to her hobbies, even the things that had served their purpose.

The top of the kneehole desk was a mess. The desk blotter, centered before the swivel chair, was considerably stained with dry, oxidized blood.

"Chest wound?" Burke said, studying the bloodstains.

"Two of them," Inspector Queen said. "One bullet through the right lung, the other in the heart. The way we put it together, she'd come in here — some time after you left, Burke — maybe intending to write in her diary, more likely to make some notes for her book of memoirs. Miss Temple says she'd been doing that before she went to bed practically every night for the last few months, and then she'd dictate the notes to Miss Temple the next day, to be typed up. Probably Glory'd just sat down at the desk when her killer showed up and shot her, most likely from the doorway there, Doc Prouty says. The angles of entry of the two bullets fired into her confirm this. The blood got on the blotter when she fell forward on being shot, as you guessed, Burke. It's a cinch she saw who shot her."

"Did she die instantly?" Ellery asked.

"No, she lived a few minutes, Doc says." The Inspector's tone was peculiar.

"Ah me and oh my," Ellery mourned. "Wouldn't it be tidy if she'd left a dying message? But that's too much to expect."

"Ask and ye shall receive," rasped his father in the same nasally mysterious way. "And may it do you a lot more good than it does us. As far as I'm concerned it could be ancient Martian."

"Don't tell me —"

"That's just what I'm doing. She lived long enough, and had enough strength — though where she got it Doc says he can't imagine, with that heart wound — to pick up a pen, or maybe she already had it in her hand, and write something on the nearest piece of paper."

44

Ellery was aquiver.

"Come over here. You, too, Burke."

They joined the old man behind Glory's desk. One of the objects on the bloodstained blotter was a police photostat of what had clearly been a sheet of ordinary lined pad-paper ("Yellow?" Ellery muttered, as if the color mattered; and his father nodded with a straight face) and roughly on one of the lines, toward the bottom of the otherwise unmarked sheet, a single word had been written.

The writing was tortured and difficult, a scrawl executed under extreme stress. The word was:

f a c e

SEVEN

"Face," Ellery said, as if he were tasting it.

"Face?" Burke said.

"Face," retorted Inspector Queen. "And that's it, gentlemen. Short, sweet, and ridiculous. It's another reason we're looking for those diaries and the manuscript of the autobiography. They might throw some light on whose face."

"Or it could be somebody's name," ventured the Scotsman. "Although I've never run across a name like Face."

"You ought to spend more time at our ball parks," Ellery said. "However, Harry, you're wrong on a different count. That *f* is definitely lowercase. No, it's got to be 'face,' as in 'face the music' —"

"Which is just what I'm going to be doing," said the Inspector, "unless we crack this thing. I've already heard rumblings from upstairs. Can't you make anything out of it, either, son?"

"No." Ellery's own face was squeezed up in a lemon-like scowl.

"Another thing." The Inspector matched the scowl; both scowling, there was a remarkable resemblance. "We still have no answer to how the killer got into the apartment. There are only two

46

keys, it seems, Glory's and her husband's. And this Armando has a real alibi, according to the West girl; also, he produced his key. Glory's apparently hasn't been touched. What's more, the apartment door seems to have been locked — there's all kinds of evidence that Glory was scared to death of burglars. So another question is, how did her killer get in?"

"Perhaps she knew who it was," suggested Burke, "and let him in — or her — herself." Then he shook his head. "No, that doesn't follow. If she'd known her assailant, she'd have written his name before she died."

Ellery was worrying it, shaking his head at Burke's last statement. He kept scowling.

"That West girl," sighed the Inspector. "I'd better talk to her personally." He called down to Sergeant Velie to fetch Roberta West. Harry Burke joined the old man at the door; the two began to whisper.

Ellery glanced at them. "Is that conference top secret?" he asked in an annoyed voice, "or can you declassify it?" They paid no attention to him.

The sorrel-haired girl came up the stairs visibly bracing herself. Inspector Queen broke off his palaver with Burke to glare at her. His glare made Burke glare at *him*. The Scot touched the girl's elbow reassuringly. She gave him a pale smile.

"I'm Inspector Queen, in charge of this case, Miss West," the old man said crustily. "I've read the reports of the detectives who questioned you, and I want to know if you have anything to add to your statement. Do you?"

She glanced at Ellery and he nodded. So she gulped and told the Inspector what she had told Ellery and Harry Burke about Carlos Armando's incredible proposal to her over seven months before.

"He wanted you to kill his wife for him," said the Inspector, perversely pleased. "That's very helpful, Miss West. Would you be willing to testify to it?"

"In court?"

"That's where people usually testify."

"I don't know . . ."

"Now, look, if you're afraid of him —"

"Wouldn't any girl be, Inspector? And then there's the publicity. I'm just getting started on my career, and the wrong kind of publicity —"

"Well, you've got time to think about it," the old man said with sudden kindliness. "I won't press you now. Velie, see that Miss West gets safely home." The girl rose, made an attempt to smile, and left with the mountainous sergeant. Harry Burke watched her slender figure twinkle down the stairs. He watched until she was lost behind the closing front door.

The old man was rubbing his hands. "That's a real development! This Armando is behind it, all right. And whoever this woman is he conned into doing the killing for him, that's the way she got in. Armando had a duplicate of his house key

48

made and provided her with it. And since she's a
woman he's undoubtedly been two-timing his
wife with, Glory never saw her before. That's
why she couldn't leave us a direct clue. She
didn't know the woman's name."

"She obviously meant something by that word
'face,' " argued Ellery. "So there must be something about the woman that Glory knew, or
spotted —"

"Something about her face?" exclaimed Burke.

"No, no, Harry," Ellery said. "It's not anything like that, or she'd have specified. Face . . ."

"Have you anything on the time she was shot,
Inspector?" Burke asked.

"As it happens, we can place it to the minute.
There was a small electric clock on her desk
there, a leather job her left arm must have
knocked off the desk as she slumped forward,
because we found it on the floor, to her left, with
the plug pulled out. That stopped the clock at
11:50. No, the clock isn't here now, Ellery; it's
at the lab, though it won't tell them any more
than it's told already. Ten minutes to twelve was
the time she stopped those two bullets. Incidentally, Doc Prouty's finding as to the time of
death jibes roughly with the clock."

"In connection with that," Burke said, "I just
remembered that as I was leaving here Wednesday night, Mrs. Armando remarked to me that
she was expecting her husband home a little past
midnight."

"That means," said Ellery slowly, "at the time

49

she was shot, Glory knew Armando would be walking into the apartment in a matter of minutes."

"He found her," nodded the Inspector, "between fifteen and twenty minutes past twelve. If he left the West girl's apartment at midnight, by the way, that would just about check out."

"It also clears up one aspect of the clue Glory left," mused Ellery. "Knowing she was dying, knowing her husband would almost certainly be the first to discover her body, she realized that he would also be the first to see any dying message she could leave. If she wrote down something that accused or described his accomplice, or involved him, he would simply destroy it before notifying the police. So —"

"So she had to leave a clue that would trick Armando into thinking it had no bearing on her murder?" Burke had taken out his pipe and was loading it absently from a Scotch-grain pouch.

"That's right, Harry. Something obscure enough to fool Armando into ignoring it — perhaps as the start of one of the word-game puzzles she was eternally doing; after all, why should he figure it was a clue? — and still provocative enough to make the police follow it up."

"I don't know," Burke said, shaking his head.

"It's too damned bad she didn't leave something good and plain," grumbled the Inspector. "Because all her fancy last-minute figuring turned out to be unnecessary. When she did die she fell forward among the papers on the desk, and the word she'd written on the top paper was hidden by her head. Armando probably didn't notice it at all — he'd sure as shooting keep his hands off that body! According to the story he tells, he never even set foot in the den — just stood in the doorway, saw the blood and his wife lying over the desk, and went right to the bedroom phone to call the police. And, you know, I believe him."

"All of which," said Ellery pulling on his nose, "gets us back to where we started: Just what did she mean by 'face'?"

"That's not where we started," his father retorted. "We started with those missing diaries, and where they are; and while, strictly speaking, it's none of your business, I'm soft-headed enough to ask both of you: Where are they?" He poked his head out the study doorway and bellowed down, "Velie! Anything on those diaries yet?" And when the sergeant's glum negative was bellowed back, the old man pulled his head back in and almost pleaded, "Any suggestions?"

The two younger men were silent.

Finally Harry Burke said, "The killer — or Armando before he phoned the police — could have taken them from the apartment."

"Not Armando — he didn't have time enough. The woman, maybe." Then the old man shook his head. "It wouldn't have made sense, though. *All* the diaries? *All* the biographical material? And don't forget, mere possession would be as

51

dangerous as a fingerprint. Incidentally, talking of fingerprints, there aren't any except Armando's, Glory's the maid's and the secretary's, Jeanne Temple's; and the maid and the secretary sleep out."

"Then they're here somewhere." Burke sucked on his pipe quietly, the very figure of a proper British police officer. "Those bookshelves, Inspector. Have the books on them been individually inspected? It occurs to me that the diaries may have false and misleading covers —"

"You mean disguised as a set of my son's books, for instance?" Ellery winced at his father's tone. "Well, they're not. That's the first thing I thought of."

"Has anything been removed from this room?" Ellery asked abruptly.

"Lots of things," said his father. "The body, the clock —"

"That's two. What else?"

"The piece of paper she wrote on."

"And that's three. Go on."

"Go on? Go on where? That's all, Ellery."

"Are you sure?"

"Of course I'm not sure! Velie!" the Inspector shrieked. The sergeant came thundering upstairs. "What's been taken from the study here?"

"The body," began Sergeant Velie, "the clock —"

"No, no, Sergeant," Ellery said. "Something not apparently connected with the crime."

The sergeant scratched his head. "Like what, for instance?"

"Like a three-step ladder," said Ellery. "As I recall her, Glory Guild wasn't more than five foot six. These bookshelves are eight feet tall. She'd need a little ladder to reach the top shelves; I can't see her dragging a very expensive monstrosity like that elephant-hide chair over to the shelves every time she wanted to reach a book over her head, or risking her neck standing on the swivel chair. So, Sergeant, where's the ladder?"

Burke was staring at him. The Inspector's mustache had lifted in a puzzled smile. Velie's mouth hung open.

"Shut the flytrap, Velie, and go get it," said the Inspector mildly; and as the sergeant left, shaking his big head, the old man said, "I forgot about the ladder. There was one in here, all right, but a detective borrowed it yesterday to look over the Dutch shelving in the dining room downstairs and didn't bring it back. Why do you want it, Ellery. We've examined everything on the top shelves."

But all Ellery said was, "We'll see."

Sergeant Velie lumbered back with a library-type ladder of ivory-decorated blackwood, with plastic-covered risers that had been scratched and scored by heavy official shoes. Ellery said, "Sergeant, would you get that pedestal out of the way?" and when Velie had moved the Watusi warrior to one side, Ellery set the ladder down where the pedestal had been standing and mounted to the top step. His hair nearly brushed the ceiling. "The loudspeaker," he explained. "I noticed that the inset of the speaker in the bedroom was screwed into the frame, whereas this one has hinges and a winged nut to hold it closed. Didn't your crew look up here, dad?"

For once the Inspector had nothing to say, although he glanced at Sergeant Velie, who paled.

"I say!" Harry Burke said. "You have a pair of eyes, Ellery. I missed it completely."

Ellery spun the nut parallel to the frame and began to pry at the inset of the loudspeaker. He got a purchase, and the inset swung out on its almost invisible hinges. "Well," Ellery said, pleased. His arm disappeared in the opening. "Just the sort of gimmicky hiding place a puzzle addict like GeeGee would think of." His arm reappeared; he flourished a metal box of the safe-deposit type. "Here you are, dad. I'll be very much surprised if what you're looking for isn't in these boxes."

EIGHT

There were six identical metal boxes in the hiding place, none of them locked; each was crammed with diaries, manuscripts, and other papers. In one of the boxes lay a kraft paper envelope sealed with wax, with the typed inscription: "My Will. To Be Opened by My Attorney, William Maloney Wasser." This envelope the Queens set aside, hunting through the boxes for the current diary.

Ellery found it, and opened it at once to the December entries. The last entry was under the date of Tuesday, December 29, "11:15 P.M.," the night before Glory Guild Armando's murder. The Inspector pronounced a salty word. She had evidently not got round to penning an entry for the day of the night she was shot; this was confirmed, as Ellery pointed out, by their having found the diary in her loudspeaker cache rather than on her desk.

All the entries were written with a fine-line pen in a tiny, precise script. A peculiarity of the dead woman's chirography was that the script looked more like italic letterprinting than ordinary writing. The individual letters were not only slanted but unjoined as in the word *f a c e* of her dying message, which Ellery also pointed out. There was very little spacing between lines, so that with the separation of the letters of individual words on the one hand, and the closeness of the lines on the other, the whole effect was at once scattered and crowded-looking. It made for difficult reading.

They skimmed through the diary from the earliest entries, page after page, and found an omission. Except for the pages date-printed *December 30* — the day of her death — and *December 31*, the only page not written on at all was the page for *December 1*.

"December first blank," muttered Ellery. "Now why didn't she write an entry for that day?"

"Why? Why?" the Inspector said, annoyed.

"Did anything unusual happen on December first?" asked Burke. "I mean generally?"

"Not that I recall," the Inspector said. "Anyway, why would that have stopped her? Unless she was sick or something."

"Inveterate diary writers don't let sickness stand in their way," Ellery said. "They almost always go back afterward and fill in. Besides, as far as I can tell," — he riffled the pages of several of the other diaries — "she kept a daily account faithfully for years. No, there's a reason for this blank page, and it hasn't anything to do with illness or oversight." He stopped suddenly. "Of course!" And he fished in his pocket and landed his cigaret lighter.

"What are you going to do, Ellery?" demanded Inspector Queen, alarmed. "Watch that flame!"

Ellery had doubled the diary back on its spine, leaving the blank page dangling, and he was carefully passing the flame of the lighter under the page.

"Invisible ink?" said Burke. "Oh, come, Ellery."

"Considering her tricky mind," Ellery said dryly, "I beg to differ."

Still, even to Ellery's astonishment, something began to appear on the blank page. The entry seemed to consist of a single word; try as he would with the flame, no other writing showed up.

Then they were staring at it:

f a c e

handprinted in the same spidery italic fashion, with spacing between individual letters, as in the case of the dying message, except that this *f a c e* was more surely written.

"Again." Ellery glared at it. "She wrote that same word on December first! In her *diary*. Now why would she have done that four weeks before she was murdered?"

"Unless she had a premonition of her death," Burke suggested.

"She must have had a lot more than a premonition," Inspector Queen said irritably, "to have written it in invisible ink." Then he threw up his hands. "Why am I always stuck with the nut cases? Magic ink! The next thing, it'll be rabbits out of a hat!"

"Very possible," Ellery said. "It seems to be that kind of rabbity business."

"Isn't it common in the States, talking about show business," murmured Burke, "to nickname theatrical personalities? Bing Crosby, The Voice. Betty Grable, The Legs. And wasn't there a star — what was her name? Marie McDonald — you people called The Body? Has there ever been one called The Face?"

"If there has been, I missed it," Ellery said. "Anyway, Harry, I point out again that in both cases — the dying message and this invisible-ink diary entry — the word is spelled with a lowercase *f*. No, it's nothing like that. Face . . ." Then he said, "Dad."

"What?"

"Was there anything unusual about Glory's face?"

The old man shrugged. "Just a face. They all look the same dead."

"I think I'd like to see this one.'"

"Be my guest." And they left Inspector Queen seated gloomily behind GeeGee Guild's desk, beginning to leaf through the diaries.

NINE

In the taxicab on the way to the Morgue, Ellery said, "Now that we're out from under the frosty eye of my father, Harry, how about telling me what you and he were putting your heads together about?"

"Oh, that." Burke seemed abstracted. "I didn't want to mention it before I checked it out with your old man —" he smiled briefly "— I'm in a strange country, remember, and one should learn the protocol of the natives. But he says it's all right."

The Scotsman squirmed back in the cab. "It has to do with the case that brought me here in the first place. Miss — Mrs. Armando's original request to the Yard was to ask if they would find a certain girl, a niece of hers, Lorette Spanier. Since it wasn't either a criminal or a missing-persons case, simply a question of locating a relative whose whereabouts she didn't know, the Yard had no jurisdiction and Commissioner Vail recommended me for the job, as I told you. I made the financial arrangements with Miss Guild — damn it all, I cannot think of her as Mrs. Armando! — with a transatlantic phone call, and went to work."

The background for his search, Burke explained, had been ordinary enough. Glory's family back in Minnesota were dead; her sole surviving relative, a younger sister, had married a British dairy farmer and gone to live in England. Both the sister and her husband had been killed in a plane crash many years before, during a summer holiday; they had left an only child, a daughter, who would now be in her early twenties.

"It seems that Glory was never very close to her sister," Burke said, between spurts of pipe smoke, "according to what she told me — disapproved of the sister's marriage, that sort of thing — and she simply lost track of the sister's daughter. Now she wanted to find the girl."

"Just like that," Ellery murmured. "Sounds as if she were looking for an heir."

Burke took the pipe out of his mouth. "You know, that never occurred to me. It might have been her reason at that."

"How did Glory communicate with the Yard?"

Burke stared. "By letter. Vail turned it over to me. For heaven's sake, what difference does it make?"

"Airmail?" asked Ellery.

"Of course."

"When did the letter come in, do you recall?"

"It arrived on the fourth of December."

"Even more interesting. Possibly significant. The page with the hidden word 'face' in the last diary is dated December first, and Glory's letter

60

about finding her niece got to the Yard on the fourth. Which means she must have written that word invisibly about the same time she wrote to England."

"You mean there's a connection between 'face' and the niece?"

"I don't mean anything, unfortunately," Ellery said sadly. "I'm just scrounging around among the possibilities. Did you find the girl? I take it you did."

"Oh, yes."

"Where?"

Burke grinned. "In New York. Ironic, what? I traced Lorette Spanier from an orphanage in Leicestershire — in the Midlands — where she'd been brought up after her parents' death, to a flat on your West Side, just a couple of miles from her aunt! And I had to come all the way from England to find her.

"The only difficulty I had was on the home grounds — it took me several weeks to trace her to the orphanage. There they told me where she had gone, although they didn't know her specific address or what she was doing — having reached her majority she was a free agent, and the orphanage people had no further control over her movements.

"When I got to New York I promptly enlisted the aid of Centre Street, which shunted me off to your Missing Persons Bureau, who could do nothing for me because the girl wasn't listed as missing anywhere in the States. And then, somehow, I got to your father. Does Inspector Queen have a finger in *every* New York police pie? He seems more like an omnibus than a man."

"He's a sort of all-purpose vacuum cleaner," Ellery said absently. "Lorette Spanier. Is that spelled with one *n* or two? And is she married?"

"One. And no, she's quite young. I think twenty-one. Or — no. By now she's twenty-two. Old enough to be married, I grant you, but there's something awfully virginal about her. And anti-male, if you know what I mean."

"I don't."

"I mean she has no time for men."

"I see," said Ellery although he didn't, quite. "What does she do for a living?"

"When she first got to the States she took a secretarial position — there was a vogue in your metropolis about that time, I understand, for pretty young English secretaries. But that was merely to keep body and soul together. What Lorette really wanted was to get into show business, she told me. She has a good voice, by pop standards, with a rather distinctive style."

"Anything like Glory's?" Ellery asked suddenly.

"A good deal like it, I'm told, although I don't qualify as a pop music buff. I'm more of a Handel-Mendelssohn-choral-society-oratorio bloke myself."

"Heredity," Ellery mumbled.

"What?"

"It apparently runs in the blood. That must

have pleased Glory no end. Has the girl broken in anywhere?"

"Yes. She managed to get a few wireless commercial jobs. It encouraged her to quit her situation and try to earn her living singing full time. She's had a few third-class nightclub dates — barely scrapes along, from what I gather. She's an independent sort — no complaints, stiff upper lip, smiling through, that sort of bilge. I couldn't help but admire her grit, though."

"Why did she come to the United States?"

"Really, Ellery. Isn't this where the pounds and pence are? Look at the Beatles." ("You look at them," said Ellery. "No, thanks," said Burke.) "She's a most practical young woman."

"Then it wasn't to look up her famous aunt?"

"Heavens, no! She means to do it on her own."

"Didn't she make any attempt at all to find her mother's only sister?"

"She told me she had no idea where Glory Guild was living. It might have been in Pago-Pago, for all she knew. No, this was all apparently coincidence."

"Not so coincidental. Where else would a Glory Guild live? And where else would a stagestruck girl come? Were you present when they were reunited?"

"Oh, yes. But getting them together took a bit of doing. I told Lorette why I'd been hunting for her, and I found myself with another job on my hands — I mean persuading her to visit Mrs. Armando."

"When did all this take place?"

"I didn't actually locate Lorette until late afternoon of the thirtieth — Wednesday. Took her to dinner and spent most of the evening talking her into coming with me. She has no particular feeling for her aunt — the woman was just a name to her as a child, and when her father and mother died — what with Glory's silence — even the name faded out after a bit. She was very young, you know, when she had to go into the orphanage."

"Bitter?"

"I beg your pardon?"

"Did Lorette seem bitter at her aunt's neglect?"

"Not at all. She's a quite remarkable young person, this Spanier girl. She said she couldn't imagine why her aunt wanted to find her after all these years. All she wanted was to be let alone to make her own way. As I say, it took me the entire evening to talk her into accompanying me. The fact was, I didn't know why Mrs. Armando wanted to see her so suddenly, either, so I had to muster some remarkable arguments."

Ellery laughed. "So that's what you and dad were being cosy about." Then he stopped laughing. "Just when did you and the girl get to Glory's apartment Wednesday night, Harry?"

"About a quarter to eleven." Burke's pipe had gone out, and he looked around the cab for a place to deposit the dottle. But the ashtray was missing, and he stuffed the whole thing in his

64

pocket. "It was awkward. Lorette was no help at all; after all, the woman was a total stranger to her. And Mrs. Armando made a bad job of explaining to the girl why she had never looked for her before, such a bad job that I decided I was in the way, and left. My assignment was finished, anyway. Mrs. Armando saw me to the door — gave me my check, by the way; I'd of course phoned her we were coming, and she had the check ready for me — and I was out of there, as I've told you, at 11:05 or so. Went to the airport, took off at 1:00 A.M. — and turned around and flew back, as you know, when Inspector Queen cabled me to return."

"Then you left the Spanier girl alone with Glory," Ellery said abruptly. "And Glory was shot at 11:50."

"I understand Lorette says she left, too, long before that," Burke replied. "She's been questioned, your father told me, and her story seems to put her in the clear. But she's going to be questioned again later today, I gather, so you can sit in and judge for yourself."

TEN

"Which one do you want to see today, Mr. Queen?" asked the attendant.

"Glory Guild Armando, Louie."

"That one." The man went straight to one of the drawers and pulled it open. "There's been quite a run on her."

She was unlovely even for a corpse. The body was almost shapeless with fat; the death-darkened, sagging cheeks under the disordered bottle-blond hair were puffy and swollen by overindulgence.

"Sic transit Glory," murmured Ellery. "This was once a sex-pot, inspiring dreams. Would you believe it?"

"With difficulty," said Harry Burke. "I don't see anything remarkable about her face, Ellery, except grossness. No mark or bruise, certainly."

"Then it wasn't her own face she meant."

"Who said it was?"

"You never know. What was it the poet said? 'A face that had a story to tell. How different faces are in this particular!' But he also said, 'Some faces are books in which not a line is written, save perhaps a date.' "

"Which poet?"

"Longfellow."

"Oh."

"*Hyperion. Not* from the fragment by Keats."

"I'm relieved," said Burke gratefully. "Well, nothing is written in this face but obesity."

"I don't know," Ellery said suddenly. "Thanks, Louie. Harry, come along."

As he hurried Burke out, the Scot said, "Where to now?"

"The Medical Examiner's office. I just had another thought."

"Minus poetic quotation, I hope," Burke said.

"I'll try to remember to spare you our native bards."

They found Doc Prouty eating his lunch at his desk. The old-timer had his disreputable cloth hat far back on his bald head, and he was making faces at a sandwich.

"Oh, Ellery. Tomato and lettuce again. By God, I've told that woman of mine a thousand times a man in my line of work doesn't necessarily have to be a vegetarian! What's on your mind?"

"The Armando case. By the way. Harry Burke, Dr. Prouty." The Medical Examiner grunted, continuing to masticate. "You've done the p.m. on her, I take it?"

"Yes. Didn't you see the report?"

"No. Anything?"

"Death by gunshot, as advertised. What did you expect?"

"Hope."

" 'That very popular trust in flat things com-

67

ing round!' " murmured Burke.

"What?" said Ellery.

"Dickens," said Burke. "Charles."

Doc Prouty was gaping at them.

"Did you look into her mouth, Doc?"

"Did I what?"

"Look into her mouth."

Now Burke stared.

"Of course I looked into her mouth. It's primary standard procedure when you're looking for poison. Not that poison was indicated," said Doc Prouty. "But then I'm the very model of a proper thorough M.E. Gilbert, W.S." He grinned like an elf.

"What did you find?"

"What I expected. Nothing."

"No wad of paper?"

"Wad of paper?"

"Wad of paper."

"Of course not!"

"And that's that," Ellery said to Burke as they left. "I don't understand," Ellery Burke complained.

"It's simple enough. Face — mouth? I thought perhaps she wrote the word face as a clue to look in her mouth — where, hopefully, she'd secreted a more direct message, like the name of her killer. Only she hadn't."

All the Scotsman could do was shake his head.

ELEVEN

They stopped in at a chophouse haunt of Ellery's, consumed vast T-bone steaks — Burke ordered his well done, to Ellery's horror — and then went back to the Queen apartment for a few hours' nap. Before they flopped Ellery sought the phone and located his father at police headquarters where, the old man said, he had conveyed the diaries and other papers.

"When are you intending to question Lorette Spanier, dad?"

"Five o'clock."

"Where?"

"Why?"

"I want to be present."

"I asked her to come down here to headquarters."

"Have Armando there, too, will you?"

The old man was silent. Then he said, "Any particular reason?"

"Nothing spectacular. I want to watch them together. The presumption is that they've never met."

"The Spanier girl and Armando?" The Inspector seemed startled. "She's hardly dry behind the ears. Fresh out of an English orphanage."

"Armando goes for anything that fills out a sweater, according to Roberta West. Does Lorette fill out a sweater?"

"Oh, yes."

"Then have Armando there."

"All *right*."

"Incidentally, has anything been done yet on the women in Armando's tasty life?"

"I started a check on that," said his father grimly, "first thing."

"The reason I ask is that the woman he got to do the job for him might be someone he knew and then — presumably — dropped. He's had platoons of them. Or she might even be one of his ex-wives."

"I'm way ahead of you, son."

But if there was anything between Carlos Armando and Lorette Spanier they concealed it like paid-up members of Equity. Armando seemed puzzled, in an amused way, by his summons to Inspector Queen's office; and Lorette after one swift look, lifted her unplucked eyebrows and ignored him. Ellery did think that, for a girl as naive as her background made her appear, it was a singularly sophisticated appraisal; but then he half dismissed it as an instinct for character analysis often displayed by the very young female of the species. As for Armando, his glance kept going over her like a dentist's probe. She filled out her sweater — it was actually a sweater — with the greatest of ease.

Lorette had nothing of the pinchy English

70

look that might have been expected from her Midlander father. She was all Norse, busty and blond; she might have come to the Inspector's office directly from a Swedish cruiseboat. (And, like the struggle her deceased aunt had so fulsomely lost, in her middle years she would have to fight the good fight against overweight.) The girl had the face of an angelic child, with a little straight nose, blue blue eyes, red red lips, and a skin as fair as an infant's backside. The pouting set to her lips had been fashionable for a long time; it was the requisite touch of sex in the child-face, and it would remind men of the woman her body said she was. Armando's eyes kept probing her, smiling with pleasure.

Armando was not at all what Ellery had expected. He did not have the lean lizard grace and greasy hair-oil look of the patented gigolo. His body was muscular and even squatty, and it moved with clumsiness. His hair, crisp, curly, and dry, was very nearly Negroid; his skin, pitted and burned black by sunlamps, enhanced the Negro impression. He possessed a pair of extraordinary black eyes, swimming with intelligence, and shaded by feminine lashes. Only his mouth was weak, being pretty and full-lipped and entirely without character. What women saw in him Ellery could not imagine. He loathed the fellow on sight. (And at once realized the source of his loathing: Armando exuded sexual self-confidence from every pore — which was perhaps what women saw in him after all.)

71

Inspector Queen made the introductions (Armando barely acknowledged the two men with a lazy *"Buon giorn' "* in a deep coo, like a pouter pigeon; Lorette shook Ellery's hand, serious and stiff-armed, a once-up-and-down pump, and then dimpled at Harry Burke, immediately illuminating the dingy headquarters office as if a shade had been raised to the sun), and sat them all down — Ellery took a chair in a corner, from which he could watch them unobserved — and said smoothly, "I've asked you here, Mr. Armando, because this is a matter that evidently concerned your wife, and I think you're entitled to know what's going on. Did you know, by the way, that Mrs. Armando was having her niece searched for?"

"Between GeeGee and me," said Carlos Armando, "there were no secrets. She told me." Secretly, Ellery doubted it. The man was improvising.

"How did you feel about it?"

"I?" Armando pulled down his pretty mouth. "I was sad. I have no family except two uncles behind the Iron Curtain, and they are probably dead." His liquid eyes washed over Loretta gently. "Miss Spanier is much to be condoled. To find such as GeeGee, and to lose her, both in the same night, is an irony so deplorable it is better not discussed."

Lorette glanced at him curiously. His blunt, brilliant teeth shimmered in a smile that dropped at the corners — punctuation marks to the extravagant foreign turn of his phrasing — while his eyes went over her in the universal language; could she be unaware of what he was? Ellery could not decide.

As for Inspector Queen, he dismissed Armando with a grunt and turned to the girl. "Mr. Burke brought you to Mrs. Armando's apartment at a quarter of eleven Wednesday night. She was home alone. Mr. Burke was with the two of you until a few minutes past eleven. Tell me as exactly as you can remember what happened after Burke left."

"Nothing *happened* while I was there, Inspector Queen," Lorette said in a reproving tone.

The old man showed his dentures in a reproved way. "I mean, what did you and your aunt talk about?"

"Oh. Well, she wanted me to come live with her, give up my flat and move in with her and Mr. Armando. I thanked her and said no, thank you, that I valued my independence, although she was very kind to ask me. You see," the English girl said, looking down at the hands in her lap, "I spent the better part of my life living with other people; you don't get much privacy in an orphanage. I tried to explain to Mrs Armando — to Aunt Glory — that for the first time in my life I was enjoying going it *alone*. And that, besides, I didn't know her. Really at all. It would have been like moving in with a stranger. I think she was hurt, but what else could I say? It was true."

"Of course," the Inspector murmured. "And

73

what else did you two talk about, Miss Spanier?"

"She wouldn't let it go at that. She seemed to have some sort of compulsion. It was quite awkward for me."

Lorette raised her amazing blue eyes. "She even . . . well, it seemed to me she went rather too far. She kept *pressing* me. She had a great many connections in show business, she said; she could help my theatrical career no end, and so on. I frankly didn't see what that had to do with my living with her — if she wanted to help me, why didn't she just do so? She was offering me a carrot, as if I were some sort of donkey. I didn't like it at all."

"And you told her so?"

"Oh, no, that would have been rude. I don't believe in that sort of tit for tat, do you? People are too self-centeredly unkind to one another as it is. I simply said that I preferred to make my own way, just as I understood she had done in her own career, and anyway I don't believe that people can boost other people in the arts — you either have talent, in which case sooner or later you'll get there, or you simply don't, and that's that. It's truly the way I feel."

"I'm sure it is. And I'm sure you're right," said the Inspector. You're a treacherous old hypocrite, Ellery thought admiringly. He caught Burke's eye; the Englishman was trying not to grin. "And that was the sum and substance of your talk with Mrs. Armando?"

"Yes."

"What time did you leave your aunt's apartment?"

"About 11:30, I should think."

"She saw you out?"

"Yes, to the lift. I mean, elevator."

"Did she say anything about seeing you again?"

"Oh, yes. She asked me to telephone her next week, something about having a spot of lunch together at Sardi's. I didn't promise. I said I would if I could, and I left."

"Left her alone — and alive."

"Certainly!"

"Was there anyone in the lobby when you went down?"

"No."

"Where did you go after you got downstairs?"

"I went home." The implications of Inspector Queen's questioning had begun to make her angry; the pink flushing her cheeks was the color of anger, and the breasts under the sweater had risen noticeably. (Most noticeably by Carlos Armando, whose eyes quivered like mercury seeking a balance, never leaving her chest.) "Where else would I go at that hour, Inspector?"

"Just asking," the Inspector said. "I suppose you took a taxi?"

"I did *not*. I walked. Is there anything wrong with that?"

"Walked?"

"Across Central Park. I live on the West Side —"

"There's something definitely wrong with

that," the old man said. "Hasn't anyone told you that it's dangerous for an unaccompanied girl to walk through Central Park at night? Especially near midnight? Don't you read the newspapers?"

"I suppose that was idiotic of me," Lorette admitted. She has spirit, Ellery thought, and the quick temper that goes with it. Also, surprising in a girl of her age and background, considerable self-control; she was now speaking with great care. "But I was not so much upset as — well — stirred up. I'm afraid I wasn't thinking clearly. I just suddenly felt like walking, across the Park was the direct route, and so I walked across. Inspector, I don't see what any of this has to do with my aunt's death — I mean, how I got home Wednesday night!"

"Did you meet anyone you know on your walk?"

"No —"

"Or in your building?"

"*No.*"

"And, as I understand it, you live alone?"

"That is correct, Inspector Queen." The blue eyes flashed. "As for what I did when I arrived at my flat — I'm sure that's your next question! — I undressed, tubbed, brushed my teeth, said my prayers, and went to bed. Is there anything else I can tell you?"

Ellery grinned at the expression on his father's face. The Inspector liked to keep on top of his opponent during these wrestling matches, and this one wasn't playing the game. The old man's dentures showed in something like respect.

"Did your aunt mention anything to you about her will?"

"Her will? Why should she have?"

"Did she?"

"Certainly not."

"Mr. Burke tells us that, as she was showing him out that night, Mrs. Armando said something about expecting her husband back a little past midnight." Mrs. Armando's husband shifted his attention for an instant from Lorette's sweater to the old man's mustache; then it went back again. "Did you hear her say that, Miss Spanier?"

"No, but she made the same remark to me after Mr. Burke left."

"But you never did see Mr. Armando Wednesday night?"

"I've not laid eyes on Mr. Armando until today." Or vice versa? Ellery wondered. If it was true, Armando was certainly making up for it now. The laying on of eyes was becoming positively obscene. Lorette did not seem to notice. She was concentrating on her inquisitor.

She waited now for Inspector Queen to resume, but she had to swivel her head.

"Question," Ellery said suddenly. "After Harry Burke left the Armando apartment, Miss Spanier — while you were alone with your aunt — did she receive a telephone call, or a message of any kind? Or did anyone ring the apartment bell?"

"We were not interrupted in any way, Mr. Queen. Of course, I can't say what may have happened after I left."

"Can you recall Mrs. Armando's remarking anything — at all — to you, no matter how trivial-sounding, that had to do with somebody's face?"

"*Face?*"

"Yes, face."

The girl shook her blond head. She seemed genuinely mystified. "I don't remember any such reference."

"Then I think that's all, Miss Spanier," said the Inspector, rising. "By the way, I take it you've heard from your aunt's attorney, William Maloney Wasser, about the reading of her will?"

"Yes. I'm supposed to be at his office directly after the funeral Monday."

He nodded. "Sorry to have broken into your New Year's Day."

Lorette rose and rather haughtily made for the door. Somehow Carlos Armando was there before her, hand on the knob.

"Allow me, Lorette — you will not mind if I call you Lorette? After all, I am your uncle."

The fine brows over the blue eyes drew together a little. "Thank you, Mr. Armando."

"Oh, but not Mr. Armando! Carlos."

She smiled faintly.

"May I drive you home? Or wherever you are going?"

"That's not at all necessary —"

"But we must know each other. Perhaps you will let me give you dinner? There are so many things about GeeGee you must be wishing to learn. Now that she is dead, so soon after finding you, I feel a responsibility . . ."

That was all the three men heard before the door closed.

"Skirt-chasing blighter," Harry Burke said, making a face. "Doesn't waste time, does he?"

"It could be," muttered Ellery, "that someone's being awfully clever."

2   HALF FACE

Physiognomy . . . may also serve us for conjecture.

LA BRUYÈRE

TWELVE

Ellery opened his eyes to a creeping gray Saturday morning. His father was gone, and in the study Harry Burke was going through the morning newspaper.

"You were pounding the feathers so hard I hadn't the heart to wake you," Burke said. The Scotsman was dressed and pinkly shaved, he had made the daybed and the pot of coffee on Ellery's electric plate was bubbling. "I've been up for hours."

"Didn't you sleep well?" Ellery made for the coffee pot like a man dying of thirst. He had slept in fits, dreaming over and over of a faceless face topped by Glory Guild's dyed hair, until, with daylight prying at the venetian blinds, he had fallen asleep from exhaustion.

"Like a side of beef," Burke said cheerfully. "That's a sleeping man's bed. My only complaint is that I couldn't find any tea in the kitchen cupboard."

"I'll pick some up today."

"Oh, no," the Scotsman protested, "one night is imposition enough. I'll put up at a hotel."

"I won't hear of it. You may have to hang around for some time, Harry, and you're no longer on an expense account. New York hotel bills have a way of escalating."

"This is terribly kind of you, Ellery."

"I'm a terribly kind person. What's in the paper?"

"Nothing we don't know. Although there's some background stuff on Armando in one of the columns."

"Whose?"

"Kip Kipley's."

Ellery set his cup down and grabbed the newspaper. He knew the Broadway columnist well; on numerous occasions Kipley had given him valuable tips. This morning's column was devoted almost entirely to the late Glory Guild's count; Ellery could imagine Armando baring his magnificent choppers. "Most of this is pretty much public property, Harry, but I have an idea Kip's holding back the real pay dirt for later developments. It gives me a thought."

He consulted his address book and dialed Kipley's unlisted number. "Kip? Ellery Queen. Did I get you up?"

"Hell, no," said the columnist's famous piping voice. "I'm in the middle of breakfast. I was wondering when you'd get around to me, Charlie. You're in this GeeGee business up to your belly button, aren't you?"

"Just about. Kip, I'd like to see you."

"Any time. I keep open house."

"Privately."

"Sure. One o'clock at my place?"

84

"You have a date." Ellery hung up. "You never know," he said to Harry Burke. "Kipley's like that wine horn of Thor's, inexhaustible. Give me twenty minutes, Harry, and we'll have brunch and hit Kip for the inside scoop."

THIRTEEN

The columnist was a tiny dark vibrant man with the profile of a doge, dressed in a heavy silk kimono of authentic manufacture. "Excuse the negligee," Kipley said, shaking Ellery's hand limply. "I never get dressed before four o'clock. Who's this?"

Ellery introduced Burke, who submitted to a quick examination by a pair of birdy black eyes. Then he was dismissed with, "Harry Burke? Never heard," and Kipley nodded toward the elaborate bar, where his Puerto Rican houseman was hovering — because of Kipley's column, Felipe was probably the most advertised houseman in Manhattan. The penthouse apartment was almost sterile, unfeminine to the bone; Kipley was a notorious hypochondriac and woman-dodger, with a housewife's passion for order. "What'll you have to drink?" He was also a non-drinker.

"Too early for me, thanks," said Ellery and Burke, sensing a clue, declined as well, although he eyed the Johnnie Walker Black Label longingly. Kipley nodded to Felipe, and the houseman vanished. It seemed to Burke that the columnist was pleased.

"Park it, gentlemen. What do you want to know?"

"Whatever you've got on Carlos Armando," Ellery said. "And I don't mean that warmed-over rehash you ran this morning."

The columnist chuckled. "It's all in the timing, Charlie; I don't have to tell *you*. What's in it for me?"

"Nothing I can think of," Ellery said, "at the moment. Because as yet I don't know a thing. If I come up with anything I can let you have, Kip, you'll get your *quid pro quo*."

Kipley looked at him. "I take it Mr. Burke here is all right?"

"Harry's a private detective, from London. He's connected with the case in a peripheral sort of way."

"If you'd rather, Mr. Kipley, I'll leave," Burke said without rancor. He half rose.

"Sit down, Charlie. It's just that when I spill my girlish secrets I like to know who-all's on the bugging end. So this thing has a British tie-in? Who?"

"Who's spilling whose girlish secrets?" Ellery asked, laughing. "Come on, Kip, open up. I told you we have a deal."

"Armando." Kipley pulled his Venetian nose. "The guy is strictly a no-goodnik. A sex-crazy maniac. And greasy as the top of a one-arm short-order cook's stove. The way he slimed up GeeGee's nest for over five years — with that stupid middle-age canary never suspecting a

87

thing, as far as I know — is enough to make even me puke."

"He's been two-timing her?"

"Your arithmetic stinks, Charlie. Two times whatever he can lay his itchy hands on, which is every broad within reach. He even gets nostalgia every once in a while."

"What do you mean?"

"Goes back to one of his rejects. For instance, he's been spotted recently in some night spots with Number Seven on his hit parade — the wife before GeeGee, the Chicago meat-packing dame who got the goods on him while he was giving it to the upstairs maid and kicked him out without a dime, which was a real switch. You know, Mrs. Gertie Hodge Huppenkleimer — she dropped the Armando when she got the divorce. Gertie's living in New York now, in a fifty-thousand-a-year pad on Beekman Place, and somehow he's managed to shinny his way back into her good graces. Don't ask me how he does it. Of course, there isn't a woman who can see beyond the end of her panty-girdle; even so, life isn't all beddy-bye. What do they see in that jock? Unless he's found a way Krafft-Ebing or Kinsey missed."

"The question is, what does Armando see in Mrs. Huppenkleimer?" Harry Burke put in. "While I was still on duty for the Yard, Ellery, I saw her at one of the Queen's garden parties. She has the physique of a Beefeater, topped with three-foot hats. Perhaps it's a matter of professional pride with Armando — I mean, not having succeeded in tapping her the first time round."

"That could be his weakness," Ellery nodded. "Who else, Kip?"

"I'm not through with his ex-wives. He's been seen squiring Numbers Three and Four — Three was Mrs. Ardene Vlietland, the one they call Piggyback, who divorced Hendrix B. Vleitland the banker, to marry Armando — *that* one broke up after that brawl in Newport where the guests were swinging from the crystal chandeliers and throwing horseshoes at everything breakable, including two Picassos. Four was that Boston dame, the alcoholic with the race horses, Daffy Dingle; she went AA and stayed on the wagon four years, and Armando's been seen in Boston bistros here and there buying her vodka martinis by the quart — just for the hell of it, I guess."

"Nice chap," Burke muttered.

"The best," said Kipley.

"The Huppenkleimer, Piggyback, Daffy," said Ellery. "Three ex-wives. I take it you haven't exhausted the inventory, Kip?"

"Get set for this one," said Kipley.

"I'm quivering all over."

"GeeGee's secretary," said Kipley. "What's-her-name — Jeanne Temple."

"Ah, me," said Burke.

"Oh, my," said Ellery. "This one *is* rancid. And damned dangerous for him. Or is he the complete fool? Under Glory's nose, Kip?"

89

"No, this he's played cosy. He's got a kind of animal cunning that pops out once in a while. With Jeanne Temple it's been hideaways around town. Not too often. Only a dirt-hound like me would have nosed it out."

"I haven't met the Temple woman. Is she anything to look at?"

"A pair of boobs surrounded by the usual number of arms and legs. With a face like a stepped-on egg. According to my information, he's got her tongue hanging out."

"Our mammary culture," murmured Ellery. "The poor European infected with the American disease. Anyone else?"

The columnist said, "I've hardly started."

"I'd better take notes!" He actually produced his notebook and began writing.

"A two-bit would-be actress named Roberta West." Burke paled slightly. "No money in her, but she's young and pretty — I guess the count needs relief every once in a while from the dogs. But he hasn't been seen with the West number for six, seven months, so that one's probably broken off." Ellery and Harry Burke exchanged glances. "What's the matter, did I say something?"

"No," said Burke.

Kipley's black eyes narrowed unpleasantly. "You two wouldn't be holding out on me, would you?"

"Yes," Ellery said. Burke looked positively unhappy. "But we don't have the right to go into that, Kip. Anyway, the West girl's connection with the case will probably break soon. Who else?"

The columnist jotted something down on a pad at his elbow. "I didn't furnish this joint out of official handouts, Charlie. Thanks for the tip. . . . Well, there's Marta Bellina."

"The opera singer?"

"In person. Bellina was probably GeeGee's best friend. Armando's been crawling all over the best friend, too, and if Marta minds she's been keeping it a deep, dark secret. Women!"

"Incredible," Burke muttered.

"Marta Bellina," Ellery wrote. "Next?"

"Her doctor."

"Whose doctor?" Ellery asked, glancing up.

"GeeGee's."

Ellery looked startled.

Kipley laughed. "If Armando's a faggot he hasn't been caught at it. No, Dr. Merckell is a lady doctor — Susan Merckell, M.D."

"The Park Avenue laryngologist who's so popular with show people?"

"The same. Handsome woman; never married. Made to order for the count. All he has to do is fake a sore throat, go to Dr. Merckell's office, and get into her examining room. My information is that during Armando's visits it's the doctor who gets examined."

"Where do you dredge up all this muck?" asked Harry Burke in a disgusted voice.

"Do I ask you where you plant your bugs,

91

Charlie?" the columnist asked amiably. "Then there's the broad with the veil."

"What?" exclaimed Ellery.

"He's been seen in the company of a chick who always wears a violet veil. A thick one, so you can't make out her face."

"Always?"

"Always."

"How old is she?"

"Can you tell a femme's age nowadays when you can't see her puss? If the sun stopped coming up and all the power failed, there'd be one hell of a lot of happy grandmas."

"How about the veiled woman's hair?"

"Sometimes it's blond, sometimes it's red, sometimes it's brunette. But it's the same woman in my book. With wigs . . . I see you two are interested in Madame X. As interested as I am. Basically, Armando is stupid. Letting himself be seen around town with a veiled dame! She might just as well be wearing a topless bathing suit. Don't you ever read my column?"

"Not as often as I'm going to from now on," Ellery said fervently. "By the way, have you any idea when Armando was last seen with the mysterious veiled woman?"

"Before Christmas, I think. You ask like pushy questions, man. What's the date got to do with anything?"

"It's just an idea I'm working on. Is there anyone else?"

Kipley said simply, "I've run out."

Ellery signaled to Burke. "Kip, I can't tell you how grateful I am —"

"You can take your gratitude and you know what. Give me some poop, Charlie, and we're brother Elks."

FOURTEEN

They went down to police headquarters and spent the remainder of the day going through page after crammed page of Glory Guild's diaries and memoirs. For the most part the diary entries were inconsequential — guests entertained, parties attended, weekends spent; reactions to first nights, an occasional acid comment about a pop singer. The diaries were sequined with name-dropping references to the great and notorious of show business, as if the late GeeGee had never entirely outgrown her Middle West clothes. There were surprisingly few allusions to her husband, and not a syllable about Carlos's relationships, real or imagined, with other women. Either Glory Guild had been unaware of his woman-chasing or she had chosen to ignore it, at least for the record.

There was no clue in the entries to what she might have meant by "face." Nor any mention of a veiled woman; nor even of a veil, violet or any other color.

Close examination of her memoirs — the typed parts and the notes on which they were based — proved equally barren of any references that might remotely connect with the singer's death.

A glance at Inspector Queen's reports advanced nothing; they told less than both men already knew. The Inspector's detectives had turned over some stones and discovered various crawly things — Armando's renewed alliance with ex-wife Number Three, Ardene Piggyback Vleitland, her of the Newport catastrophe; his affairs with his wife's secretary, Jeanne Temple, and with her physician, Dr. Susan Merckell; his duet with the opera singer, Marta Bellina. But there were no reports on Number Four, the Back Bay alcoholic, Daffy Dingle, or on Number Seven, Gertie Hodge Huppenkleimer, Glory Guild's immediate predecessor.

Or, significantly, on the veiled woman.

"We'll get after *her* first off," the Inspector said, "and I'll give Boston a call about the Dingle woman. I'm most interested in this purple-veil dame —"

"Violet," said Ellery gravely. "It could make all the difference."

"Get off my leg," his father snapped. "I'm not much interested in Mrs. Huppenkleimer. She's the only wife Armando wasn't able to take for anything. I can't see a woman like that committing murder for him."

"Still, according to Kipley, she's been going out with him again. Why?"

"Who knows why women do what they do? Maybe she's been overcome by fond memories. You chase after her if you want."

"Which is exactly," said Ellery, "what Harry and I are going to do."

They tracked Gertie Huppenkleimer that night to a charity ball at the Americana. She stood out like an atom bomb in the New Mexico desert — a towering mushroom of a woman who dominated most of the thousand glittering people in the ballroom.

"Suppose I make the approach," murmured Burke. "Gertie has a thing for Englishmen."

"You're a Scotsman."

"Believe me, old chap, she won't know the difference."

Ellery watched Burke maneuver his broad shoulders toward the punch table, where Mrs. Huppenkleimer was bellowing into the ear of a captive African diplomat. A few minutes later the Scotsman was dancing with her, fitting neatly under her hat. And a few minutes after that he was back.

"Nothing to it, Ellery. We have a breakfast appointment with her for tomorrow morning. She was charmed."

"By what?"

Burke grinned. "I told her we'd met at the Queen's garden party. I could have had her bra after that. Although, come to think of it, what the hell would I use it for?"

"A hammock," said Ellery glumly, eyeing her awesome proportions.

They were admitted to the Beekman Place duplex at 11:00 o'clock Sunday morning by an English butler who actually sported sideburns. Madam, it appeared, was awaiting them; they followed the butler to a glassed-in terrace, where Mrs. Huppenkleimer was enthroned in an enormous basket chair before a breakfast table set for three.

"Mr. Burke, how very *nice!*" their hostess roared. "And this is your friend. I'm so happy to meet any friend of Mr. Burke's; . . . Ellery Queeg, did you say? . . . *Queen.* How gauche of me! Please sit down, Mr. Queen! And, of course, you, Mr. Burke . . ."

Burke launched into British social chitchat skillfully while the butler served from a king-sized steam table. Mrs. Huppenkleimer ate on the same enormous scale as the rest of her; quantities of wheatcakes, shirred eggs, sausages, kippers, toast, and coffee disappeared down her maw. Ellery, insinuating a phrase or two here and there to keep his ear in, found himself thinking of Moby Dick — she was vastly dressed in billowing white. Was Carlos Armando some sort of Captain Ahab, pursuing her out of complex notions of vengeance — bending her to his will to the ultimate point of slaughter? Or was he more like the Man-Frog Mowgli riding Hathi the Elephant to their mutual satisfaction?

"Oh, yes," Harry Burke was saying to her. "I've also run into Count Armando. Oh, dear, I suppose I shouldn't have mentioned him, Mrs. Huppenkleimer. Weren't you and the count once married?"

"I was, and as a count he's a phony, and there's no reason why you shouldn't, Mr.

Burke," the woman said, reaching for a cigaret with her flipper. Burke hastily snapped his lighter to the ready. She puffed, nodded, belched, and sank back in the basket chair. "Dear Carlos is such a transparent fraud," she laughed, shaking all over. "But one can't stay mad at him. You know? Such a gallant. Though I don't think he's ever quite forgiven me for having a photographer present when I caught him with that maid. I was joking with him about it only the other night."

"Really?" said Burke. "You're seeing him again, Mrs. Huppenkleimer? I think that's awfully decent of you. Letting bygones be bygones, I mean, and all that."

"Why shouldn't I see him again? There's nothing Carlos can get out of me that I'm not willing to give him, is there? Of course," she said thoughtful as a cow, "with this mess he's in I may have to drop him for good. We'll see." She reached for a piece of cinnamon toast that had escaped her earlier and began to masticate it, the cigaret smoldering between the heavily jeweled fingers of her other hand. "I certainly can't afford to become involved."

"You mean in his wife's death?"

"I mean in his wife's murder," the woman said grimly, and flicked the crust to the fat blond cocker waiting for it.

Ellery had a sudden revelation. Gertie Huppenkleimer, in spite of appearances, was nobody's fool. For one thing, she had kept switching her glance on and off him all the while she was talking to Harry Burke — not inquiringly, but as if she had known all along who "Ellery Queeg" was.

He made a decision.

"I'm afraid we've eaten your delicious breakfast under false pretenses, Mrs. Huppenkleimer," Ellery said. "What we're doing here is investigating Mrs. Armando's murder." Burke looked pained.

"Everybody tries to take advantage of poor me," Gertie said calmly. "Go ahead and investigate — Mr. What-Was-It? I haven't a thing to hide."

"Queen," Ellery said. "I'm glad you haven't, Mrs. Huppenkleimer, because that makes it easier for me to ask you where you spent the half hour before midnight of this past Wednesday."

"The night before New Year's Eve. Let me see . . . Oh, yes! I attended a United Nations reception for the new ambassador from whatever-it-is, some Southeast Asian country. Afterwards a group of us went down to one of those places — what do they call them? disco-something — the one on Sheridan Square, in the Village."

"What time did you leave the U.N. reception?"

"About 10:30." The shrewd eyes, imbedded in fat, took Ellery in. "Am I suspected in the Guild murder? That would be too funny."

"What's funny about it, Mrs. Huppenkleimer?"

"Why would I want to shoot Carlos's wife? To marry him again? Once was enough, thank you. He amuses me, and I'm perfectly satisfied with the present arrangement, or I was until this thing came up. The whole idea is ridiculous."

Suddenly, it was.

"You went directly from the reception, in a group of people, to Greenwich Village?"

"That's correct."

"Did you leave the discothèque at any time?"

"No, Mr. Queen." She was smiling a big fat smile.

"And at what time did the Village party break up?"

"After three in the morning. Sorry to disappoint you." The smile was swallowed by abdominal laughter.

"This business is mainly disappointments, Mrs. Huppenkleimer. We'll have you checked out, of course."

"Of course." She was still laughing at him. But when she turned to Harry Burke, it was with a gargantuan baby pout. "As for you, Mr. Burke, shame! I really fell for that Queen's garden-party line, and I don't mean Mr. Queen."

"Oh, I was there," said Burke gallantly. "Keeping an eye on the jewelry."

"And you would have made such a wonderful lord." Mrs. Huppenkleimer sighed. "Hawkins" — what else could her butler be called? Ellery thought — "show these gentlemen out."

They found Jeanne Temple in an apartment building on East 49th Street where, from the card under the bell in the lobby, she shared an apartment with a girl named Virginia Whiting. It

100

consisted of one bedroom, a kitchenette, and a living room; the bedroom and kitchenette were tiny, the living room large. The apartment was nondescriptly furnished and in bachelor-girl disorder. Both girls were dressed in Capri slacks and jersey tops; both were barefoot. The Whiting girl, who was rather pretty, had vivacious gray eyes; but Jeanne Temple was a plain mouse, her only attribute of note being an astonishing bust which taxed the jersey to its limit.

"No, I don't mind Virginia's being present," the Temple girl said. She looked thirty, although Ellery suspected she was younger. There was fear in the muddy brown eyes behind the aluminum-frame glasses. "In fact, I'd rather she . . ."

"Take it easy, Jeannie," said the other girl. "You've got nothing to worry about."

"I know it," Glory Guild's secretary burst out, "but *they* don't seem to. Why can't you people let me alone? I've told everything I know —"

"Not everything, Miss Temple," Ellery said.

The droopy skin yellowed. "I don't know what you mean."

"I'm referring to you and Carlos Armando."

The yellow began to burn. "Me and Carl—Count Armando?"

"Your relationship with him."

"What do you mean?" she asked excitedly. "Did he tell you — ?"

"Our information is that you and Armando were having an affair behind Mrs. Armando's back."

"That's not true."

101

"I'm afraid it is. You've been seen with Armando in hideaway restaurants and bars, Miss Temple, on a number of occasions. Men like Armando don't take their wives' secretaries out secretly in order to give them dictation."

"Miss Temple," said Harry Burke gently. "We're not interested in blackening your reputation. What we're after are the facts."

She was silent, the hands in her lap clutching each other. And then she looked up. "All right, we've been having an affair," she said faintly. "I . . . I don't know, really, how I got into it. It just seemed to happen. I've tried to break it off, but he wouldn't let me. He's kept threatening me, saying he'd see to it I lost my job. I haven't known what to do. I like — liked my job, and Mrs. Armando paid me well, and treated me nicely, well, most of the time . . . I've felt so guilty . . . He wouldn't let me alone after that first time . . ."

"We know what a swine he is," Burke growled.

Ellery frowned at this unprofessional remark. But it seemed to do something to Jeanne Temple, as if she sensed that Burke was an ally. After that she addressed all her answers to him, in a sort of gratitude. Virginia Whiting sat quietly by; of course she had known about the affair — Jeanne could hardly have kept it a secret from her.

Ellery said abruptly, "Did *you* know Carlos Armando, Miss Whiting?"

The gray-eyed girl was surprised. "Me? Hardly!

I've seen him in the apartment here — twice, I think. But it was only for just long enough to get out of the way and go to the movies."

He found himself rather liking her.

"Did he ever make a pass at you?"

"Once, while Jeannie was getting her face on in the bathroom," Virginia Whiting said grimly. "I've been taking karate lessons, and I gave him a sample. He didn't try it the second time."

Jeanne Temple's mouth was open. "You never told me that, Virginia."

"There's a lot of things I've never told you, Jeannie. Including what a patsy I thought you were to let that wolf get his paws on you in the first place."

"I know," Jeanne said, "I know what a fool I've been."

"Did Armando ever say anything about marrying you?" Ellery asked her.

"No."

"I mean, if you got rid of his wife for him?"

Her eyes flashed at that. "Certainly not!" she cried. "What do you think I am, Mr. Queen? Is that what the police are thinking?"

"The thought," said Ellery "has crossed a few minds. He never made such a proposal? Even hinted at it?"

"*No*. And if he had, I'd have — I'd have gone straight to Mrs. Armando and told her everything!" She was trembling. Virginia Whiting took her hand, and she began to cry.

"I'm sorry if I've upset you, Miss Temple.

There isn't much more. How did you spend the evening of December thirtieth — last Wednesday?"

"But I've been all through that with the detectives —"

"Let's go through it once more, shall we?"

"I'm Jeannie's alibi," said the Whiting girl calmly. "We had dinner together that evening. Neither of us left the apartment — I'd turned down a date because I had a big one coming up the next night, New Year's Eve. Jeannie and I watched television together all evening. We saw the 11:00 o'clock news, then part of the Johnny Carson show. It was a few minutes past the 12:00 o'clock break when we turned the set off and went to bed. At the same time. Together."

"Miss Temple didn't leave the premises at any time Wednesday night?"

"She did not. Neither did I, so I'm in a perfect position to know."

"That would seem to be that." Ellery rose, and Burke followed suit. Jeanne Temple was swabbing her eyes. "Oh, one other thing, Miss Temple. Does the word "face" mean anything special to you?"

The girl looked blank. "Face?"

"You know, face? *f-a-c-e?*"

"I can't imagine what you mean."

"Do you recall Glory Guild's ever making a point of anyone's face? Around December first? More recently? Particularly on Wednesday?"

The secretary shook her head. "Mrs. Armando certainly never remarked about anyone's face to me. As a matter of fact, she was always rather vague about people's features; she never knew what color anyone's eyes were, things like that. She was nearsighted, and for some reason couldn't wear contact lenses, and she didn't use her ordinary eye-glasses except for reading or working. She was rather vain, you know. She did notice women's clothes, that sort of thing, but —"

"Thank you, Miss Temple."

"That mucker," Harry Burke muttered in the taxi. "There ought to be special laws for men like Armando. So you could get a court order to have him altered, like a dog."

"He does have a way with women, doesn't he?" said Ellery absently. "If only we could get a lead to what she meant."

"What who meant?"

"GeeGee. By that word she wrote. It might explain everything. It *would* explain everything."

"How can you know that?"

"It's a feeling I have, Harry, in my northern-most bones."

FIFTEEN

Dr. Susan Merckell proved disconcerting. She was entertaining some people in the huge Park Avenue apartment behind her street-level office, and she was openly annoyed at the Sunday interruption. "I can give you only a few minutes," she said in a brusk voice as she led Ellery and Burke to a study. "Please say what you have to say, and let me get back to my guests." She was a small woman with an hourglass figure, blunt unfeminine hands, and very little makeup. But her simply coifed blond hair was natural, and her lips were almost grossly sensual. It was not hard to think of her as a physician; she had the medical stamp of authority. "What is it you want to know today? I've already been questioned."

"Your exact relationship with Carlos Armando," Ellery said.

"I've already answered that one." Her hard green eyes did not change expression. "Count Armando was the husband of one of my patients. He's come to me for treatment himself on several occasions. Next question?"

"I'm not through with the first question, Dr. Merckell. Have you ever had any relationship

106

with Armando that might be called nonprofessional?"

"If you think I'm going to answer that, you're an imbecile."

"Our information is that you have had."

"Does your information include proof?" When Ellery did not reply, Dr. Merckell smiled and rose. "I thought not. Will there be anything else?"

"Please sit down, Doctor. We're not through." She shrugged and sat down. "Do you recall where you were Wednesday night? The night before New Year's Eve?"

"I was at Park Center Hospital."

"Doing what?"

"I was called into an emergency consultation."

"Who was the patient?"

"A man with a laryngeal carcinoma. I don't remember his name."

"Who called you into consultation?"

"A g.p. named Krivitz — Jay Jerome Krivitz. There was also a surgeon present, Dr. Israel Mancetti."

"At what time Wednesday night, Doctor, did this consultation take place?"

"I got to the hospital about 11:00 o'clock. The consultation lasted over an hour."

"You mean it was after midnight when you left?"

"What else can I mean? Over an hour from 11:00 P.M. makes it after midnight, yes. Really,

107

gentlemen, you're wasting my time and making me neglect my guests." Dr. Merckell rose again, and this time it was evident that she had no intention of resuming her chair. "I've been asked these questions before, as I told you."

"But not by me," said Ellery. "Doctor, does the word 'face' convey anything significant to you?"

The green eyes gave him a mineral stare. "I'm a laryngologist, not a dermatologist. Is it supposed to?"

"I don't know, I'm asking. Can you recall Mrs. Armando's ever mentioning anything about someone's face, or faces in general?"

"You're either drunk or irresponsible. Even if she had, how could I possibly remember anything as trivial as that? Good day, gentlemen!"

SIXTEEN

Marta Bellina was in Los Angeles, they discovered, giving a concert.

So they went to police headquarters where, not surprisingly and Sunday notwithstanding, they found Inspector Queen floundering in a swamp of reports.

"Nothing," the old man grunted. "Not a blasted thing anyone could call a development! What did you two find out?"

Ellery told him.

"Well, then it all washes out. I've already checked the Huppenkleimer woman's whereabouts on the night of the murder —"

"I thought you weren't interested in Huppenkleimer," Ellery said with a grin.

"— just for exercise," his father snapped, "and it checks with what you say she told you. The Temple girl is given an alibi by her roomie, as you just found out. Boston has cleared ex-wife Number Four, Daffy Dingle — what a name for a grown woman! — who suddenly committed herself to a nursing home in Springfield last Monday to take the cure from all those vodka martinis Armando's been pouring down her guzzle; she hasn't set foot from the premises since she went in. Ex-wife Three, Ardene Vleitland has been with friends on a yacht cruising the Caribbean since last Saturday; I've had the Coast Guard check on the yacht, and it hasn't put in to a port since it sailed. That takes care of the ex-wives Armando's been diddling around with. And my report on Dr. Merckell confirms her consultation alibi at that hospital."

"What about the opera singer?" asked Harry Burke.

"Marta Bellina is in L.A."

"We know that, Inspector. But where was she last Wednesday night?"

"In San Francisco. She's been on a concert tour for the past three weeks and hasn't been back to New York since. We did an especially careful job on Bellina because in this jet age how far is New York from anywhere? But, according to the information we've received from the California authorities, her alibi stands up."

"Leaving," mumbled Ellery, "the woman in the violet veil. Dad, what have you got on her?"

"A big fat nothing. Your friend Kipley seems to have it down pat. The last time a woman of that description was seen with Armando was just before Christmas. If he's been out with her since, we can't get a make on it."

"Leaving," Ellery mumbled again, "the woman in the violet veil."

"Stop saying that!"

"I have to. She's the only woman Armando's

been seen with who hasn't an alibi for the night of the murder."

"Unless," said Burke, "you find her and she does have."

"Okay, so she's a possibility as his accomplice," growled Inspector Queen. "So are a hundred other women, for all I know. With Armando's magic touch with the more foolish damn fools among the opposite sex, we could be on this case until NASA lands a man on Venus."

Their last interview that day was with the magician himself. They found Armando in his widow's Park Avenue duplex with a weak bourbon and water in his manicured hand, the TV set tuned to the Ed Sullivan show. He did not offer them a drink. He did not even ask them to sit down.

"Alone at the boob tube, Count?" asked Ellery. "I expected to find some lady with a *Playboy* center spread holding your hand, condoling with you."

"Peasant," said Carlos Armando. "Am I never to be rid of you louts? My wife is to be buried tomorrow, and you torment me! What do you want?"

"I could ask you for the secret of your allure, but I'm afraid such secrets aren't transferable. Who's the woman in the violet veil?"

"I beg your pardon?"

"Oh, come, Armando," said Harry Burke. "You're not playing ticky-tack-toe with a lot of gullible females. Among your various other en-

111

terprises, you've been squiring some wench in a violet veil. Quite openly, which makes you more stupid than I think you are. We want to know who she is."

"You do."

"You can understand English, can't you?"

"You will never force one word about the lady from my lips," Armando said profoundly. "You are all boors where women are concerned, you Anglo-Saxons." ("Highland Scottish in my case, old chap," Burke murmured.) "That is why your attempts at fornication and adultery are so pitiful compared with the techniques of European men. We Europeans know what women want; you know only what *you* want. And what women want, secondly — I do not have to tell even you what they want firstly — is not to have their names thrown about in delicate affairs. I have heard American men discussing their conquests in locker rooms, clubhouses, and over brandy and cigars as if the women involved were street whores. I spit on your questions." He actually pursed his pretty lips.

"Bully for you," said Ellery. "But, Carlos, this is not an ordinary conversation. Or affair. Your wife is dead by shooting, and not accidentally, either. And you engineered her departure —"

"I of course reject that utterly and absolutely," Armando said hotly. "It is slanderous and insulting. I point out to you that when my wife was shot I was visiting in the apartment of Miss West. I wish I had a non-interested witness here

112

so that I might sue you for defamation of character. Alas, I have no such witness. I can only ask you to leave my premises at once."

Neither Ellery nor Harry Burke moved.

"He's a beauty, isn't he?" said Burke. "Sheer brass, and a yard deep. Tell me, Count, are you as much of a man with your trousers buttoned? I'd like nothing better than to square off with you and find out."

"Are you threatening me, Mr. Burke?" Armando asked in an alarmed voice. He glanced quickly at the nearby telephone. "Unless you leave at once, I shall call the police!"

"I'm half tempted to let you find out how much good that would do you," Ellery said. "Was the woman in the veil the love-nest birdie you charmed into shooting your wife for you, Armando? Because we're going to find her, I promise you that."

Armando smiled. "The best of luck to you in your search, my friend," he said softly.

Ellery stared at him, puzzled. Then he said, "Come on, Harry. I need fresh air."

SEVENTEEN

"Where are we going?" Roberta West asked Harry Burke.

The Scot said shyly, "I had a thought, Miss West. I hope you'll like it."

He had phoned her on impulse late Sunday evening, after parting from Ellery and had not only found her in but in a mood for company. They had had a late dinner in a hole-in-the-wall Italian place on Second Avenue, candlelit, with Chianti from a wicker bottle with a three-foot neck.

The taxi hit 59th Street and turned west. The streets were beautifully empty. It was a brisk, star-prickled night.

Roberta glanced at him curiously. "You seem awfully excited."

"Perhaps I am."

"By what, may I ask?"

"Oh, something." Even in the dark she could have sworn that he was blushing. He added in a rush, "By you, for example."

The girl laughed. "Is that a sample of the latest British line? Over here it went out with the bustle."

"It's *not* a line, Miss West," Burke said stiffly.

"I've been too busy to learn any."

"Oh," Roberta said. And they were silent until the taxi pulled up in the plaza. Burke paid the man off, helped Roberta down, and waited until the taxi drove away. "Now what?" Roberta asked expectantly.

"Now this." He took a delicate hold on her muskrat-covered elbow and steered her to the first of the three horsedrawn cabs waiting at the curb. "An amble around your park. That is . . . if you'd like?"

"What a scrumptious idea!" Roberta squealed, and hopped in, to be enveloped by the wonderful odor of horse, old harness, and oats. "Do you know something?" she exclaimed as the Scot pulled himself up beside her and began fussing with the lap robe. "In all the time I've been in New York, I've never taken a ride in one of these things."

"Do you know something?" Burke mumbled. "In all the time I've been in London, I never have, either."

"You mean you've never been in a hansom cab?"

"Never."

"How wonderful!"

Later, while the carriage was clopping along in Central Park, being whooshed at by passing cars, Harry Burke's hand fumbled under the robe and found Roberta's.

Her hand was correctly cold, but she let him hold it.

Still later, on the return swing of the journey, he leaned over and, in an act of sheer desperation, pecked about for her lips and ultimately located them. They felt like rubber gaskets.

"Can't you do better than that, Miss West?" Burke muttered.

In the dark he heard her giggle. "Under the circumstances, Harry, don't you think the least you could do is call me Roberta?"

Only when he had left her outside her apartment building — she was quite firm about his not escorting her upstairs — did Burke realize that she had failed to demonstrate whether she could or could not do better.

He sighed not unhappily. He rather thought she could, and he rather thought she would.

In time.

EIGHTEEN

It is universal police procedure to stake out detectives at the funeral in a murder case, on the magnetic theory that the murderer will be drawn to his victim for the last possible time. Inspector Queen dutifully had his men at the Long Island cemetery. Ellery passed the departmental rites up; he lacked the traditional police mentality. As far as he was concerned, he knew the murderer — if not in deed, then in inspiration; besides, he had no stomach for Armando's play-acting this morning. And it was beyond belief that the woman in the violet veil would put in an appearance. Armando would see to that.

"He might have telephoned to warn her off," Harry Burke said over their late breakfast. "Haven't I heard rumors about an occasional discreet official wiretap in your marvelous country?"

"I see no evil and I hear no evil," proclaimed Ellery from behind a mouthful of scrambled egg and Canadian bacon. "Besides, I doubt Armando would be so careless. If I gauge our boy correctly, Violet Veil has had her orders for a long time. I'm much more interested in today's will reading."

"Who's going to be there?"

"The only one we haven't met is Selma Pilter — Glory's old manager. Which reminds me, Harry. We'd better try to get a make on her."

He reached for the extension phone on the cupboard and dialed a number.

"Felipe? Is there any chance that Mr. Kipley is out of the hay? This is Ellery Queen."

"I go see," said Felipe noncommittally.

"*Marvelous* country," Burke murmured, glancing at his watch.

The columnist's voice shrilled in Ellery's ear. "God damn it, man, don't you ever sleep? What's with the Guild case? A break?"

"I'm afraid not. I just need some information."

"Some more information, you mean. When do I get my *pro quo?*"

"In time, in time, Kip," Ellery soothed him. "Do you have anything on Glory's manager? Selma Pilter?"

"Do I have anything on the Sphinx? Not a speck of dirt, if that's what you're after. And if you think the count's been tossing Selma around, forget it. Even he draws a line. She's an Egyptian mummy."

"How old is she, Kip?"

"Four thousand, if you've got twenty-twenty. In her sixties, if you're blind. She used to be a singer herself. A long time ago. Never made it, quit, and turned to the percentage racket. Damned good at it, too. She made Glory a millionaire."

"I know that. Is there anything else about her I ought to know?"

"Well, she and Glory were a tight twosome. They never had the troubles most temperamental artistes have with their managers. Selma couldn't be a threat to other women, which was one reason; the other was that she's a real cool operator. What else? Aside from she keeps pretty much to herself. If she has a life of her own, she hides it under her falsies. She's a deep one."

"How do you mean?"

"Deep. Don't you understand English?"

"Thanks, Kip."

"When am I going to have to thank you, Charlie?"

They were a little early for the will-reading appointment. William Maloney Wasser turned out to be a large, portly, outwardly calm man with a polka-dot bow tie and a tic. The tic seemed to fascinate Harry Burke.

"No, I can't say I knew Glory Guild really well," the lawyer said as they waited for the funeral party in his office. "My dealings with her were mainly through Selma Pilter — who, by the way, is one of the smartest businesswomen I've ever had anything to do with. It was Selma who recommended my firm to Glory when Glory was looking around for somebody to handle her affairs. Selma's steered a number of her clients my way."

"Then I take it you haven't been Glory's lawyer long?"

"About fifteen years."

"Oh. Didn't she have a lawyer before you?"

"Willis Fenniman, of Fenniman and Gouch. But old Will died, and Glory didn't like Gouch — she used to say they didn't make music together." Wasser seemed more amused than irritated by the interrogation. "Do I understand, Mr. Queen, that I'm being grilled in a murder case?"

"Habit, Mr. Wasser. Forgive me. Besides, you've already been looked up. The police department has found you and your firm lily-pure and clean-o."

Wasser chuckled, and then his secretary announced the arrival of the funeral party. Before he could instruct her to show the party in, Ellery said hurriedly, "One thing, Mr. Wasser. Does the word 'face' have any special meaning for you?"

The lawyer looked blank. "Is it supposed to?"

"*F-a-c-e.*"

"You mean in the context of this case?"

"That's right."

Wasser shook his head.

NINETEEN

Carlos Armando ushered Lorette Spanier into the law office with a deference that none of the onlookers could doubt, least of all the girl. It seemed to Ellery that she was half pleased by it, the other half being annoyance. Armando actually took up a post behind her chair. She was the mystery ingredient in his ointment and, as such, had to be fingered with care. Jeanne Temple he ignored. Whether this was out of the contempt of familiarity or the discretion of broad experience Ellery was unable to decide. In any event, it was clearly a bad situation for the secretary of the dead woman. By the side of the busty child-blonde with the pout and the dimple, the Temple girl faded like an overexposed chromo. She was so aware of it that her muddy brown eyes spattered Armando with loathing before her glance lowered to the gloved hands in her lap, where it remained.

Selma Pilter produced a shock, and a downward revision of Ellery's estimate of Kip Kipley's judgment. The old woman's ugliness approached an esthetic experience, like the ugliness of a Lincoln or a Baronesse Blixen. Her fleshless frame was so fine as to suggest hollow bones, like a bird's; Ellery half expected her to flap her arms and sail to a chair. Her long face narrowed to an almost nonexistent chin; the coarse dark skin was like the bed of an extinct river with the ripple-marks showing. Her nose was a scimitar edge, her lips a multitude of hairline wrinkles, her pendulous lobes further elongated by African earrings of ebony. (Had the elephant-hide chair and the Watusi warrior in Glory Guild's den been gifts from Selma Pilter? The old woman's wrists and fingers were loaded with jewelry of African craftsmanship.) Only a sliver of dye-shiny black hair showed under the tight turban she wore. For the rest of her, her emaciation was covered by a severe suit; her throat was mercifully hidden by a scarf; her birdlike feet perched on stilted heels. But her eyes were beautiful, black and lustrous, like Carlos Armando's, and with a deep intelligence. The whole woman was somehow medieval. Ellery was fascinated by her; so, he noted, was Harry Burke.

Inspector Queen came in last; he shut the door quietly and stood with his back against it. When Ellery offered his chair in pantomime — the office was two chairs shy — the Inspector shook his head. He evidently wanted to be in a position to study every face.

"We meet here today," began Wasser, "for the reading of Glory Guild Armando's will. Two of the interested parties cannot be present — Marta Bellina, who is on a personal appearance tour on the Coast, and Dr. Susan Merckell, who

122

has been called out of state on a consultation.

"The will," continued the lawyer, unlocking a desk drawer and taking out a kraft envelope sealed with wax, "or rather this copy of it, is a true copy property witnessed and notarized." He broke the seal and drew out a document backed with blue legal paper. "It is dated December the eighth last."

Ellery recognized the envelope as the one he had found in a metal box in GeeGee Guild's loudspeaker hiding place — the envelope marked "My Will. To Be Opened by My Attorney, William Maloney Wasser." The date of the will struck him as significant. December 8 was only seven days past the date of the blank page in Glory's diary — the page to which he had applied his lighter and brought out the word "face." Something had happened on December 1 that apparently was pivotal in the retired singer's life — some event that immediately caused her to institute a search for her niece Lorette Spanier and within a week to write a new will (it was inconceivable that no previous will had existed).

He was right, for at this moment Wasser, reading from the document, was saying, "This is my last will and testament, revoking any and all wills in existence prior to this date," and so on. Whatever the result, the cause had been sufficiently alarming to prevent Glory Guild from spelling it out in her diary, and to drive her to the cryptic one-word reference in disappearing ink, an act which more and more took on the cast of desperation.

But then Ellery concentrated on the legacies.

Wasser was reading a long list of bequests to individually named charitable organizations — surprisingly picayune bequests; none exceeded $100 and most were for $25 and $50. Considering the extent of the murdered woman's estate, this opened a whole new wing of her character. She had evidently been one of those insecure people who dispense their largess diffusively, Ellery thought, to cover as many good causes as possible with the least hurt to themselves, out of some conflict between social parsimony and a hunger for praise. Armando, hovering over Lorette Spanier's shining head, seemed pleased.

But the will revealed paradoxes. There was a $10,000 bequest to "my faithful secretary, Jeanne Temple." (The faithful secretary's glance leaped from her lap to the lawyer's face and back again, the brief leap accomplished with surprise, delight, and Ellery was sure of it — shame.) "My dear friend, Marta Bellina" received a like sum (paradox now, since the opera star was rich as Croesus's wife, not only from her professional earnings but from the estates of the two rich husbands she had buried). "My physician and friend, Dr. Susan Merckell" was left $10,000 also. (Another *pourboire* to the well-heeled; Dr. Merckell's practice brought her an income in six figures.)

And Selma Pilter, "my dear friend, to whose brilliant and devoted management over the years I owe everything . . ." Ellery watched the old woman closely. But there was nothing to be seen on the wrinkled little face. Either she had supreme command over herself, or she knew what was coming. ". . . I leave the sum of $100,000." Ellery heard Armando utter something unpleasant-sounding in Italian.

Ellery leaned forward. Wasser was coming to the meat of the will, and he had paused. The lawyer seemed embarrassed, or uneasy.

"To my husband Carlos," Wasser began, and paused again.

Armando's black eyes were staring at Wasser's lips.

"Yes?" he said. "Yes!" Ellery thought it unworthy of him.

"To my husband Carlos" — the lawyer paused again, but only for a moment this time — "simply to tide him over until he can find another source of income, I leave the sum of $5,000."

"What!" shrieked Armando. "Did you say $5,000?"

"I'm afraid so, Mr. Armando."

"But this is — this is criminal! There is some mistake!" The widower was waving his arms hysterically. "True, GeeGee and I had an agreement in which I renounced my share in her estate. But I point out to you, Mr. Attorney, that in the contract it said that at the end of five years GeeGee would tear this agreement up. The five

125

years went by, and she did tear it up — before my eyes. That was almost a year ago. So how could she have cut me off with this . . . this bagatelle!"

"I don't know what you saw torn up, Mr. Armando," said Wasser uncomfortably, "but your premarital agreement with Glory Guild is still in existence, therefore in force —" he waved a paper "— here is a copy of it, attached to Mrs. Armando's copy of the will. The original of the agreement is attached to the original of the will. Both are already in the hands of the Surrogate's Court."

"I wish to see that!"

"Certainly." Wasser hastily rose, but Armando had already bounded to the lawyer's desk and snatched the paper from his hand. He scanned it unbelievingly.

"But I tell you she ripped the original of this to bits and burned them!" The man was in a panic. He muttered, "I see, I *see.* She did not actually reveal the paper to me. She merely told me it was the one, and I was stupid enough to take her at her word, and then she tore up the dummy paper . . ." A millrace of invective, in some language Ellery did not recognize (could it be Romany, the language of his allegedly gypsy background?) streamed from Armando's lips. "She duped me!" he howled. The hatred and anguish on his pitted face were Glory-directed; what was in all their minds — that GeeGee Guild had known about or suspected his continuous infidelities, so that in her eyes he had flouted their agreement

126

over and over — apparently did not, enter his. "I shall sue! I shall take this to your courts!"

"That, of course, Mr. Armando," said Wasser, "is entirely up to you. But I don't see what you hope to gain. You can hardly contest your authentic signature on this agreement; and the mere existence of the agreement past the end of the conditional five-year period is *prima facie* evidence that your wife did not consider you to have fulfilled your end of the bargain. I think you'll find that the physical evidence carries all the weight. It certainly isn't going to be overthrown by your unsupported word that she destroyed the agreement when she clearly didn't."

"I could have had at least one-third of her estate. A million dollars! My dower right! It is not to be borne!"

"In the face of this agreement, Mr. Armando, you'll have to be satisfied with the $5,000 your wife left you."

Armando seized his head and turned away. "I will get it, I will get it," he mumbled. Then he seemed to collect himself, and his pretty mouth tightened. He resumed his position behind the English girl's chair, glaring blackly into space. Ellery divined what he was glaring at. He was glaring at the irony of his act. He had engineered his wife's murder for $5,000, instead of the million he had looked forward to. Now someone else would fall heir . . . Ellery saw Armando's fiercely bitter eyes narrow as his train of thought came to this way station. Who was

GeeGee's principal beneficiary?

The lawyer read on: "I leave the whole of my residuary estate, real and personal, to my only close blood-relation, my niece Lorette Spanier, if she should be found . . ." A long paragraph followed, providing for the event that Lorette Spanier should have died prior to testatrix's death, or the alternative event that she should not have been found, alive or dead, within seven years of testatrix's death; in either instance, the residuary estate was to establish a foundation, the purpose of which was to provide scholarships and fellowships for furthering the musical careers of singers and other musicians. The formulation of the foundation was gone into in detail — irrelevant now that Lorette Spanier had been found alive and legally identified.

It was Carlos Armando who spoke first. "Congratulations, Lorette. It is not every orphan who finds herself a millionaire at the age of twenty-two." He did not even sound bitter. The count had regained command over himself. Like a good general, he wasted no time brooding over the failure of his attack. He was already making plans for the battle ahead. (Ellery thought: He must be giving himself a medal for his foresight in establishing a bridgehead to his wife's niece at their first meeting.)

As for the young heiress, she sat stunned. "I don't know what to say. Really I don't! I met my aunt only once, for less than an hour. I don't feel as if I have the right —"

"The feeling will pass, my child," murmured Carlos Armando, stooping over Lorette. "I know of no feelings that can stand up against so much money. Tomorrow, when you have thrown me out of the apartment I have occupied so long — and did you know that it is a condominium, fully paid up? — you will wonder how you could ever have been poor."

"Oh, don't say that, Uncle Carlos! Of course I shan't do any such thing. You may stay in the apartment for as long as you like."

"Do not be so generous," said Armando, shaking his head like a wise old uncle. "I would be tempted to accept, now that it is I who am poor again. Besides, our Mr. Wasser would not allow it — am I correct, Mr. Wasser? I thought so. And we could hardly occupy the same premises; it would cause the kind of talk that is so unfairly associated with my name. No, I shall take my few miserable possessions and move out to some rooming house. Do not concern yourself about my fate, *cara*. I am quite accustomed to privation."

It was a splendid performance, and Lorette Spanier was moved to tears by it.

TWENTY

As the group was dispersing, to Ellery's surprise William Maloney Wasser asked Selma Pilter and Lorette to remain. Harry Burke glanced at Ellery who gave him the nod, and Burke left with Jeanne Temple and Armando. Armando went away reluctantly.

"Do you mind if I hang around, Mr. Wasser?" asked Inspector Queen.

"Well, no," the lawyer said. To Ellery glancing at his father, it looked like a put-up job. "You don't object, do you, Mrs. Pilter?"

"I want Inspector Queen to sit in on this," said the old woman; she had a voice that seemed to come from her bird's feet, high and clear and sweet. "And Mr. Queen, since he's obviously an interested party."

"That I am," muttered Ellery.

Wasser came around and shut his office door carefully. Then he hurried back to his desk, sat down, and rubbed his heavy chin. Lorette was looking puzzled; whatever was on the lawyer's mind, the girl was ignorant of it.

"I hardly know how to say this, Miss Spanier," Wasser began. "It's an unusual situation — not a black and white matter by any means. I mean . . .

130

I suppose the only thing for me to do is lay the facts before you and let you be the judge."

"Facts?" asked the English girl. "About Mrs. Pilter?"

The old woman simply sat there, silent.

"You know, of course, that Mrs. Pilter was your aunt's trusted manager and booking agent for a great many years. I had it from Glory's own lips — and I know it out of my personal dealings with Mrs. Pilter — how very astute and absolutely scrupulous she has been in her handling of Mrs. Armando's affairs. The fact that your aunt left Mrs. Pilter that handsome legacy in her will is proof enough of her esteem and gratitude. However." He stopped.

It sounded like an ominous conjunction. Lorette glanced over at Selma Pilter in bewilderment.

"I think, Mrs. Pilter," said the lawyer, "you had better take it from there."

The ugly old woman rustled as she stirred in her chair. But her beautiful black eyes were fixed on the girl. Whatever lay behind the look, it was deeply tucked away.

"My dear, I am one of those silly, unfortunate people who have an uncontrollable passion for betting on horse races," Selma Pilter said. "Every penny I've ever saved has gone into the pockets of bookmakers. I would be a wealthy woman today if not for my weakness for gambling.

"Late last month I found myself into the bookies for a great deal of money. They're not exactly reasonable people, and I was actually in physical danger. Of course, it was all my own fault; I had no one to blame but myself. I was badly frightened. They gave me forty-eight hours to pay up, and I had not a single legitimate way of raising the money. So . . ." she hesitated; then her withered old chin came up. "So, for the first time in my life, I did something dishonest. I borrowed — I told myself it was 'borrowing' — the money from Glory's funds.

"You see," the old woman went on steadily, "I had the rationalization worked out in my mind. I knew Glory was leaving me $100,000 in her will — she had told me so. So I talked myself into believing that I was only taking an advance against my own money. Of course, it wasn't that at all; for one thing, Glory could have changed her mind about leaving me so much money. It simply wasn't mine to take. But I did. And then, a few days later, came Glory's sudden death, which was such a shock by itself, and for the other reason that I faced an accounting that would reveal the shortage. And I had no way of replacing it — I'm afraid my credit isn't very good at the banks.

"That's the situation, Miss Spanier. The legacy will more than repay the shortage, but the fact remains that I did take money entrusted to my care, and you would be entirely within your rights to bring charges against me. And that's the story."

She stopped and simply sheathed her claws.

"Not the whole story," Wasser said quickly. "I was completely unaware of the borrowed funds until Mrs. Pilter herself called it to my attention. She phoned me about it last night. And I decided to hold the matter over until after the reading of the will today.

"It's the main reason," he went on, turning to Inspector Queen, "that I called you last night and asked you to be sure to be present, Inspector. Naturally, I don't relish the prospect of possibly being accused of withholding information in a murder case, although I'm positive the information is totally irrelevant to the case. As far as the borrowed funds are concerned, of course, it's Miss Spanier's decision as to whether to press a charge or not. She's the principal legatee."

"Oh, dear," said Lorette. "I don't know you, Mrs. Pilter, but from everything I've heard you practically made Aunt Glory's career. I'm sure that if she put so much trust in you you're a basically trustworthy person. Besides, I can hardly play the role of First Stone-thrower. I saw too much misery in the orphanage —" her dimple showed "— in fact, I caused a great deal of it myself. No, I shouldn't dream of preferring charges."

Selma Pilter drew a wobbly breath. "Thank you, thank you," she said in an unsteady voice. "I'm lucky for your charity, child. I have very little for myself." She rose. "Will there be any-

133

thing else, Mr. Wasser?"

"Inspector Queen?" The lawyer looked relieved.

"If Miss Spanier won't charge her, that's it as far as I'm concerned," said the Inspector; and the Queens left.

"You know, Ellery," the Inspector said as they taxied downtown, "the Pilter woman's embezzlement could be a motive."

"It could?" Ellery sounded preoccupied.

"Knocking off GeeGee for the hundred grand legacy in order to cover the shortage."

"And telling Wasser all about it before she even collected? You can't have her covering the shortage and uncovering it in the same hypothesis."

"She could be playing this smart. For the very reason you've just given — to make herself look like the original honest woman. Meanwhile, she's off the hook with the defalcation. She knew she couldn't have kept it under wraps indefinitely. Not with a shrewdie like GeeGee Guild to account to. And Wasser doesn't seem to me a lawyer you can fool for very long. I say it's a possible motive."

"I say it's a possible nothing," Ellery said crudely. He was slumped so far down he was almost sitting on his shoulderblades. "That part of it, anyway. But there is something about Selma Pilter that bothers me."

"What's that?"

"Her face. It's certainly the outstanding face

of the century — outstandingly, outrageously, superbly ugly. So much so that it may be why Glory wrote the word down as she was dying."

"Do you believe that for one minute?" his father snorted.

"Not for a second," muttered Ellery.

TWENTY-ONE

"You certainly know how to feed a man," said Burke, lying back on the well-worn French provincial sofa.

"You certainly know how to pick out the music that goes with it," said Roberta West, sitting straight up on it.

They were spending the evening in Roberta's apartment on East 73rd Street. It was in an old elaborate building whose gentility was a bit scabbed at the edges, and its rooms had high ceilings with elaborate plasterwork, the kind of curlicued decorations that should have framed mural cupids and dryads with ash-green architectural trees and pale flat brown French horizons for background. But there was nothing in the panels except a few unframed and not very good Dufy and Utrillo reproductions. The tall windows were swoopingly draped in burlap dyed maroon, and there was an ancient Italian fireplace that had been stopped up for a generation. And since Roberta possessed very little furniture, the allover effect was gigantic, dwarfing her petite dimensions further, so that she rather resembled a redheaded Alice caught in the Shrink-Me stage.

Burke thought she looked adorable. He did not, of course, dare to say so.

She had fed him a roast beef and Yorkshire pudding dinner, "to make you feel at home," and the beef was too rare and the pudding too doughy for his taste (or anyone's, he caught himself guiltily thinking); but then a man needn't expect everything in a woman with so many exemplary points (although points wasn't quite the word); therefore the manful lie about her culinary wisdom.

As for the music, that was his contribution (aside from a bottle of undistinguished California burgundy) to the festivities. Roberta had said that she owned a modest hifi and he had stopped into Liberty's on Madison Avenue on his way uptown and bought an *Elijah*, with the Huddersfield soloists and chorus, not knowing that Roberta's small collection of records consisted mainly of Mancinis, old Glenn Millers and such, her prizes being two or three vintage Whitemans; but Burke was taking such obvious pleasure in the oratorio that Roberta had the extra wisdom to express pleasure in it, too, although most of it either mystified or bored her.

So they both lied gallantly, and it turned out a smashing evening.

Afterward, as they sat side by side on the sofa, he lolling with sternly repressed longings and she properly straight-backed, Burke murmured, "This is so comfortable. It makes a man feel like — well, like taking his shoes off."

"Don't," said Roberta, "give in to the feeling."

"Oh? Why not, Miss — I mean, Roberta?"

"Taking your shoes off could start a trend."

He blushed. This time, in the full light, she was positively bathed in it. "I didn't mean —"

"Of course you didn't, cookie," Roberta crooned. "That was bitchy of me. Take your shoes off, by all means."

"I believe," the Scot said huffily, "I'll leave them on, thank you."

Roberta laughed. "Oh, you're so — so Scotch!"

"Scottish is the preferred term."

"I'm sorry. I've never known a Scotchman — I mean a Scotsman — before."

"I've never known a young American girl before."

"Not so young, Harry. But thanks for the compliment."

"Rot. You can't be more than twenty-one or two."

"Why, thank you! I'll be twenty-seven my next birthday." Considering that she was going to be twenty-eight, Roberta did not think the fib too enormous for her conscience to bear.

"Oh! And when will that be?"

At the conclusion of the evening, as Burke stood in the doorway hat in hand, he suddenly found himself seizing her like a rapist and catching her lips before they could go into their rubber-gasket act. He was astounded by both his lust and their softness.

So it was a smashing evening to the very end.

TWENTY-TWO

Into the penthouse apartment moved Lorette Spanier, out of it went Carlos Armando — the suffering but understanding "uncle" to the end — and less than two weeks later Lorette took a companion to share the apartment with her.

Harry Burke was the catalyst.

Ellery had expected him to return to England, but the Scot lingered. It was certainly not the Guild-Armando case that was keeping him in New York; the Inspector had no further need of him, and in any event he would be a mere jet's flight away if he went home. Yet the only move Burke made was from the Queen apartment — "I can't take advantage of your hospitality indefinitely," he said, "like *The Man Who Came to Dinner*" — to a modest midtown hotel.

"It's none of my business, Harry," Ellery said to him, "but my nose is itching. Don't you have to earn a living? Or is something keeping you here that you've been holding out on me?"

"I have an associate in my office in London," Burke retorted, "who can jolly well carry on while I take my first sabbatical in years. That's one thing, chappie. For another, I feel a certain responsibility toward that girl."

"Lorette? Why?"

"A, she's a British subject. B, this is a murder case. C, I was instrumental in bringing her into the case when I located her for Glory Guild. On top of that, she's grown on me. Reminds me of a favorite sister of mine who trapped an Aussie into wedlock fourteen years ago and whom I haven't seen since. But the principal reason — I'm uneasy about her."

"Because of Armando? You needn't be. There's a man on his tail day and night."

"It's not so much Armando, although I don't like the way the mucker looks at her. I don't know, Ellery. Lorette's rattling around alone in that museum of an apartment, she's a very inexperienced twenty-two, and she's suddenly an heiress to millions. She could become the target of all sorts of nastiness."

"Well, congratulations," said Ellery with every appearance of heartiness. "It's mighty decent of you, Harry."

Burke reddened to the roots of his sandy hair. "Oh, I'm a mighty decent bloke."

Ellery did not doubt the verity of Burke's professed reasons for hanging about New York, but he suspected that Burke had another reason he was not professing. The great man's suspicion was soon confirmed. Burke was seeing Roberta West regularly. Remembering how instantly smitten the Scot had been on that New Year's morning, when the West girl had come to the Queen apartment to tell her appalling story

140

about Armando's proposal to her, Ellery was not surprised. He ragged Burke about dissembling.

"Are you checking on me, too?" Burke asked in a hard voice — a very hard voice. It was the first time Ellery had seen him angry.

"Of course not, Harry. But with so many detectives running around in the case, you could hardly keep your meetings with Roberta West a secret."

"It's no secret, old chap! I just don't like making a display of my personal life."

"Are you in love with her?"

"Nothing is sacred to you, is it?" Burke unexpectedly chuckled. Then he said soberly, "I think so. No, I'm pretty damned sure. I've never felt like this about a woman before."

"Does Roberta feel the same way about you?"

"How the hell should I know? We haven't discussed her feelings — or mine, for that matter. It hasn't reached that stage. Do you know, Ellery, you've the cheek of an overgrown Mod?"

"That opinion of me," Ellery said cheerfully, "is now transatlantic."

It was Harry Burke who got Lorette and Roberta together. He took the two girls to dinner one night, and they liked each other immediately. Afterward, they went back to the penthouse, where the girls spent the rest of the evening in intense exploration. It turned out that they had a great deal in common — their views on men, morality, Viet Nam, the Beatles, *Playboy* Magazine, Martin Luther King, bikinis,

141

Frank Sinatra, Joan Baez, pop art, and the theater generally were in delightful agreement. Best of all, to Lorette at least, Roberta had already achieved a success — in Lorette's eyes — as an actress. The blond girl's windfall fortune, it seemed, had not affected her ambition to follow in her late aunt's footsteps.

"You two were made for each other," Harry Burke said, beaming. "In fact, it gives me an idea."

The blond head and the sorrel top turned to him. In their discovery of each other, they had almost forgotten he was there.

"Lorette, you simply can't live in this huge place alone. Why doesn't Roberta move in with you?"

"Of all the gall!" Roberta gasped. "What a thing to say, Harry. I thought Englishmen were the soul of reserve."

"They are. I'm a Scot."

He beamed again.

"Why, Roberta, it's a lovely idea!" Lorette cried. "Oh, would you?"

"Lorette, we've only just met —"

"What has that to do with anything? We like each other, we have the same interests, we're both unattached — oh, Harry, that's an inspiration! Please, Roberta!"

"Golly, I don't know," the little actress said. "How does that cornball line go? This is so sudden." She giggled before she said, "Are you sure, Lorette? I'd have to sublet my apartment — my lease isn't up till October — and if we didn't get along or something, I'd have an awful time finding another place to live. A place I could afford."

"Don't worry about *that*. We'll get along, Roberta, I know we will. And another thing. It wouldn't cost you tuppence to live here. Imagine all the rent you'd be saving."

"Oh, I wouldn't dream of such an arrangement!"

"You two battle it out," murmured Harry Burke, "while I wash my hands." He had made the suggestion not hopefully, remembering Lorette's independence, her living alone on the West Side, her shyness with strangers. But apparently the grandeur of the Guild apartment had over-awed her. It was an immense place for a lone girl to rattle around in, and his suggestion of a compatible companion had come at the psychological moment. Burke congratulated himself.

When he came back, they were clinging to each other. So that was that.

Burke felt top hole about it.

As for the murder case, it limped. In spite of intensive investigation, Inspector Queen's detectives were unable to turn up a clue to the mysterious woman in the violet veil; as far as they were able to determine, she had not appeared in public again, certainly not in Armando's company. He was cultivating a fresh crop of women these days, pretty young ones for pleasure, aging ones with fat estates behind them for potential investment — all of whom were investigated with reference to Violet Veil, and all of them fruitlessly.

There was nothing to indicate that any of these newcomers to Armando's *liste d'amour* might be women he had previously wooed.

It was exasperating.

Not that the count was neglecting his past. He was also paying court to a few of his ex-wives — notably Gertie Huppenkleimer — and making an occasional phone call to the penthouse "to ask how my little niece is coming along." At such times Roberta found an excuse for leaving the room.

"I can't stand the sound of his voice. It makes me sick," Roberta said when Lorette once asked her why. "Look, darling, I know it's really not my business, but Carlos was behind your aunt's death — how can you bear to talk to him?"

Lorette was distressed. "I don't encourage him to call, Roberta, really I don't . . ."

"You do, too. By answering the phone."

"If I didn't, Carlos would come up here, possibly make a scene. I abhor scenes. Besides, I can't bring myself to believe it."

"Believe what?"

"That he planned Aunt Glory's death. I don't care what Harry Burke, Ellery Queen, and the police say. They'll have to prove it to my satisfaction first."

"Lorette, he proposed it to *me!*"

"Maybe you misunderstood him —"

144

"The heck I did," Roberta said. "Don't you believe me?"

"Of course I believe you. I mean, I believe you think he did. Oh, I know Carlos is no rose — that he's done a lot of things that aren't very nice — especially where women are concerned — but ... murder?" The blond head shook in disbelief.

Roberta looked appalled. "Lorette, you're not *falling* for him?"

"What an absurd idea." But the English girl had turned quite pink.

"You *are*."

"I'm *not*, Roberta. I wish you wouldn't even suggest it."

Roberta kissed her. "Don't you ever let that animal mess around," she said fiercely. "I know."

"Of course not," said Lorette. But she drew away from the other girl, and a little coolness settled between them. It soon lifted, but each made an excuse to go to bed early that night.

It was the first far cloud of the thunderstorm.

TWENTY-THREE

One Sunday in mid-February the girls invited Burke and Ellery to brunch. The Scot arrived at the penthouse early, with Ellery only a few minutes behind. The new maid admitted them (Glory Guild's staff had resigned in a body, on various excuses, all of them adding up to the undelivered wish to get as far away as possible from the scene of murder). Lorette and Roberta were still dressing.

When Roberta was finished she wandered into the master bedroom. "You about ready?"

"In arf a mo'," Lorette said; she was applying her lipstick. "Roberta, what a stunning cross. Where did you pick it up?"

"I didn't," Roberta said, fingering it. It was a heavy silver Maltese cross on a silver chain, and it glittered like a star. "It was a birthday gift from Harry."

"And you didn't tell me."

Roberta laughed. "At your age, darlin', you can afford to advertise. Me, I'm up in the late twenties."

"Not so late. Twenty-seven."

"Lorette! How did you know?"

"Harry told me."

"I'll never tell that man another secret as long as I live! Actually, I fibbed a bit. I'm twenty-eight."

"Oh, don't be a ninny. He didn't tell me till yesterday, and I picked something up for you at Saks."

"That wasn't necessary . . ."

"Oh, shut up." Lorette rose from the vanity and went to one of the closets. She opened the door and reached up to a high shelf piled with hatboxes; a Saks box tied with gilt cord was perched on one of them. "I'm sorry I'm late with a gift," she said, rising on tiptoe to reach the Saks box, "but it's your own fault — damn!" In pulling at the gift box she tipped over one of the hatboxes, and both boxes fell off the shelf. The lid of the hatbox came off and something distinctly not a hat came bouncing out and stopped at Lorette's feet.

"What," exclaimed Roberta, pointing, "is *that?*"

The English girl stared down at it.

It was a revolver.

"It's a revolver," Lorette said childishly. Then she began to stoop.

"I don't think you ought to touch it," Roberta said, and Lorette stopped. "Whose in heaven's name is it?"

"It doesn't belong to *me*. I've never even seen a gun so close."

"Unless . . . Is that your Aunt Glory's hatbox?"

147

"It's mine. A hat I bought only a fortnight ago. But there certainly wasn't any revolver in the box when I set it on the shelf."

They stared at each other. A disagreeable something settled over the bedroom.

"I think," Roberta said, "I think we'd best let Harry and Ellery handle this."

"Oh, yes . . ."

They went to the door together and called down together. The men came bounding upstairs.

"A gun?" Harry Burke ran into the master bedroom, Ellery at his heels. Neither man touched the weapon. They listened in silence to the girls' story of how it had been found, then simultaneously they made for the closet and examined the tumbled hatbox and the floor around it.

"No ammo," muttered Ellery.

"I wonder," began Burke, and stopped. He looked at Ellery. Ellery did not look back. He was on all fours, rump in air, examining the weapon as best he could without handling it. "What make and caliber is it, Ellery?"

"Colt Detective. A .38 Special, two-inch barrel, six-shot. Looks pretty aged to me — the plastic stock is nicked and cracked, the nickel finish looks worn." Ellery took a ballpoint pen from his pocket, inserted it in the trigger guard, and rose, balancing the revolver on the pen. Burke squinted at the gun.

"Loaded with .38 Special cartridges. Four.

148

That makes two shots fired. Glory Guild stopped two bullets." The Scot's burry voice sounded like a damp firecracker.

"You mean this could be the weapon that killed Mrs. Armando?" Roberta West asked in a smallish voice.

"Yes."

"But how could that be?" cried Lorette. "And even if it is, I don't understand what it's doing in the apartment. Did my aunt own such a weapon?"

"Not legally," said Ellery. "There's no record of a gun permit issued to her."

"Then it undoubtedly belongs to her murderer," the British girl said reasonably. "That follows, doesn't it? But it makes matters more puzzling than ever. He certainly — whoever he was — didn't leave the gun behind. Or . . . is it possible the police didn't search the apartment thoroughly enough?"

"The apartment was gone over like a bloody dog looking for fleas," Harry Burke said. "There was no gun here. That is, directly after the shooting."

Lorette's eyes burned a brighter shade of blue. "What you mean, Harry, is — before I took possession of the apartment. After all, the gun was found in my hatbox. Isn't that what you mean?"

Burke did not reply.

The silence became embarrassing.

Lorette broke it with a toss of her blond locks. "Well, the whole notion is the most silly nonsense. Surely no one would believe — ?" But then she stopped. It had evidently occurred to her that there were potential believers within sound of her voice.

Ellery slid the revolver carefully down on Lorette's bed. "I'd better call in," he said.

"Why do you have to?" Roberta burst out. "It *is* nonsense! There's undoubtedly the most innocent explanation —"

"Then nobody will be hurt." He went to the extension. "May I?"

"Be my guest," Lorette said in her bitterest Americanese. She sank onto the other side of the bed from the gun and clasped her hands between her knees, the picture of little-girl helplessness. Roberta ran out of the room. They heard her crying while Ellery waited for his father to answer the phone.

TWENTY-FOUR

The report from Fingerprinting was negative; there were no prints on the .38 Special — the usual result. But Ballistics had news for them. Firing tests and the comparison microscope had established that the bullets dug out of Glory Guild's body and the bullets fired by the Colt Detective found in Lorette Spanier's hatbox had been discharged by the same weapon. The markings were identical.

They had the murder gun.

"It's a break," Inspector Queen chortled to the two silent men in his office. "This is all we need to establish a case against the Spanier girl, as I'm sure the D.A. will agree."

"Let's hear it," muttered Ellery, "out loud."

"The girl claims Glory didn't tell her about the new will naming her principal legatee. Doesn't it stand to reason that Glory did tell her? After all, what had Glory been looking for her for? To make Lorette her heir. Is it reasonable that, after finding her, Glory *didn't* tell her?"

"They had only a few minutes alone together."

"How long does it take?" his father retorted. "Five seconds? Number one."

151

"That's hardly conclusive, Inspector," Harry Burke protested.

"I'm talking about the weight of the circumstances, Burke, as you very well know. Number One covers motive.

"Number Two: Lorette claims she left her aunt alive that night at around 11:30. But, again, we have only the girl's word for it. By her own admission no one saw her leave, no one saw her during her alleged walk home through Central Park, no one saw her when she got to her apartment house, no one saw her in her apartment afterward. She can't produce a single corroborating witness to any detail of her account of her movements. As far as the provable circumstances show, she could just as well have been in her aunt's place till 11:50, she could just as well have shot Glory and got home — however she did it, whether crossing the park on foot or taking a cab — twenty minutes or half an hour later than she says. So that's opportunity on top of motive."

"That," said Ellery, "is possible opportunity on top of possible motive."

"What are circumstantial cases but possibles and probables, Ellery? But then there's Number Three. You can't deny the evidence of this revolver. And neither can she. It's the gun that shot Glory, and that's a fact. *And* it was found in Lorette's bedroom. *And* in Lorette's closet. *And* in Lorette's hatbox in her closet in her bedroom. And all she can say about the gun is that she never saw it before and doesn't know how it got there. Just her unsupported denial.

"It's true," the Inspector said, "that we haven't been able to establish through the records that she bought the weapon — there's no record of such a gun at all — but she'd hardly buy it through regular channels, anyway, to commit murder with it. You know what a pipe it is to buy an unregistered weapon in this town under the counter. At that, we may be able to tie such an illegal sale to her. If we can, we've got her in spades.

"But even without that," and the Inspector showed his dentures, "we've got her. In my book this all adds up to a case we can get through the grand jury. What does it add up to you, my son? You look droopy."

Ellery was silent.

Harry Burke snapped, "Doesn't it strike you, Inspector Queen, that your argument makes the Spanier girl out all kinds of idiot? Why in hell should she have held onto the revolver if she shot her aunt with it? After — to use your own argument — going to the trouble of getting hold of one that couldn't be traced to her? It seems to me the very first thing she'd have done was throw the bloody thing into one of your rivers."

"That's what you or I'd have done, Burke. But you know as well as I how stupid amateurs can act when they're playing around with murder. Anyway, that's an argument for her lawyers. I can't see the D.A. losing sleep over it. And talking about the D.A., I'd better go over and drop this in his lap."

The old man took the Ballistics report and, cheerily, left.

"What do you think, Ellery?" Burke asked after a long silence.

"If you can call it thinking." Ellery looked as if he had swallowed something with a live bug wiggling in it. "I don't know, Harry. Looked at one way, it's one of those slick circumstantial cases that's all façade, like the camera side of a Hollywood set. Go behind the set and you see nothing more substantial than shoring. Still . . ."

"Well, in my view there's only one way to look at it." The Scotsman got to his feet. "With due respect for age and paternity, anyone who maintains that that girl is capable of murder just doesn't know people. The police mind — and I should know, from my years at the Yard — looks at facts, not human capabilities. Lorette Spanier is as innocent of Glory Guild's murder as I am. I'd stake everything I have on that."

"Where are you going?"

"Over to her apartment. If I judged the Inspector's expression correctly — and if I know prosecutors — she's going to need every friend she can muster. And Roberta would give me the sack if I didn't stand by the poor girl. Coming?"

"No," Ellery said glumly, "I'll hang around here."

He did not have long to wait. Less than two hours later a warrant was issued for the arrest of Lorette Spanier.

154

TWENTY-FIVE

On hearing the news, Attorney Wasser acted as if his late client's principal heiress had developed bubonic plague. With haste he recommended the services of a criminal lawyer and retreated behind a barricade of an astonishing number of appointments. The criminal lawyer, a veteran of the juridical wars named Uri Frankell, tackled the bail problem first.

It was thorny. Lorette Spanier's only substantial assets, her inheritance — aside from interim funds for maintenance of the apartment and incidental expenses — were tied up in Surrogate's Court. They would remain so trussed until the estate was settled, which might take months. Besides, a criminal could not enjoy the rewards of his crime, so until Lorette's guilt or innocence was legally established her rights to the inheritance dangled in limbo. Where, then, was she to get the collateral without whose negotiable existence bail bondsmen developed zippers on their pockets? All this, provided the arraigning judge was willing to set bail in a Murder One case to begin with.

In the end, Lorette went to jail.

Lorette wept.

Roberta wept.

Harry Burke was heard to mutter something not nice about American jurisprudence. (In fairness, he had often in his day muttered not-nice things about English jurisprudence, too.)

Frankell did not think the People had much of a case. He was confident, he said, that he could cast sufficient reasonable doubt into the minds of a jury to get the girl off. (Ellery began to entertain reasonable doubts about the wisdom of Attorney Wasser's recommendation. He distrusted lawyers who were confident in murder cases; he had seen too many unreasonable juries. But he kept his mouth shut.)

"In this one," Ellery said unhappily to Harry Burke, "I find myself with crotch trouble."

"Crotch trouble?" Harry Burke said, puzzled.

"Crotch trouble," Ellery said. "I'm hung up on the fence."

Ellery found himself unable to do much of anything in the weeks before Lorette's trial. He haunted police headquarters waiting for progress reports; he frequently visited the Guild apartment (where Roberta kept flinging herself from top to bottom of the penthouse bemoaning Lorette's fate, and her own — "I have no *right* to be living here while Lorette's in that awful cell! But where can I go?" — once even berating Harry Burke for having "talked" her into giving up her old apartment, a charge the Scot suffered in dignified silence); he went to see Lorette and came away with no improvements in her story but a gripe in his groin.

156

"I don't know what you're so bothered about," his father said one day. "What's eating you, Ellery?"

"I don't like it."

"You don't like what?"

"This whole case. Something about it . . ."

"Like what, for instance?"

"Like the way things don't hang together," complained Ellery. "Like the way loose ends keep flopping."

"You mean that face business."

"For one thing. It's important, dad, I *know* it. And I've vacuumed my brains and can't come up with a single conceivable cross-reference to Lorette."

"Or to anybody else," the Inspector retorted.

"Yes. That's right. It's a flopper. Keeps flopping. Charging that girl, dad, was premature. You ought at least to have found out what GeeGee meant by 'face' before you made the arrest."

"You find out," the Inspector said. "I've got other things to occupy my time. Anyway, it's all in the hands of the D.A. and the Court now. . . . What else?" he asked suddenly.

"Everything else. We'd been going, for example, on the assumption that the murder was Carlos Armando-inspired, with some woman doing the dirty work for him. Now it seems Lorette was that woman."

"I didn't say that," the old man said cautiously.

157

"Then you've changed your mind about Armando? He had nothing to do with his wife's murder?" When his father did not reply, Ellery said, "I still maintain he did."

"On what grounds?"

"By the pricking of my thumbs. By his general odor. By everything I've found out about him."

"Take *that* into court," Inspector Queen snorted.

"Granted," Ellery said. "But you see how tangled everything is. Did Lorette know Armando before they supposedly met for the first time here in this office — when you questioned her after the murder? If she did, was she Violet Veil? Armando's willing accomplice? That makes no sense at all. Why should she have consented to act as Armando's tool when, according to you, she knew she was inheriting the bulk of the estate?"

"You know his way with women. Maybe she fell for him, the way the others did."

"*If* she knew him beforehand." Ellery lapsed into brooding.

"Look, son," his father said. "There's a side to this we haven't touched on. Certainly we'll never be able to prove it —"

"What?"

"I'm not sure myself that money was the motive behind the murder."

"How do you mean? Are you conceding — ?"

"I'm conceding nothing. But if you want to fish around in theories, how about this one?

GeeGee Guild dropped her sister, Lorette's mother, after the sister married that Englishman. When Lorette's parents died in the plane crash, GeeGee let the kid be placed in an English orphanage instead of going over there, taking custody of the child, legally adopting her, or otherwise making herself responsible for the girl's future. That kind of cold-blooded neglect could well have made Lorette grow up hating her aunt. It could have been a festering sore that broke out when Burke took her to the Guild apartment that Wednesday night. It's even possible the girl came to New York in the first place to track down her aunt and let her have it.

"It's a theory," the Inspector went on, "with a built-in advantage. Under it Lorette could have told the truth about not knowing anything of the inheritance."

"It also raises an interesting alternate," Ellery said. "That if Lorette killed Glory Guild out of hatred, and not for the estate, then Carlos Armando could still have been plotting Glory's death through an accomplice, only Lorette beat the accomplice to it."

The Inspector shrugged. "That's certainly possible."

"If it's possible, why insist that it was Lorette who beat Violet Veil in the race to kill? Why couldn't it have been the other way around?"

"Because," his father replied, "we have no evidence that it was Violet Veil, as you call her, and we do have evidence that it was Lorette."

"The .38?"

"The .38."

Ellery fell into reverie. He had been theorizing as pure exercise. The truth was, he did not believe any of the theories. Had his father pressed him, he could not have answered why, beyond the pricking of his thumbs.

"Unless," the Inspector concluded, "Violet Veil *was* Lorette. Two motives — Armando's, for what he thought he was going to inherit, Lorette's for revenge."

Ellery threw up his hands.

TWENTY-SIX

On the day before the Lorette Spanier trial there was a meeting in the law office of Uri Frankell. It was a Tuesday afternoon, with a dirty overcast and a threat of snow.

The lawyer, who looked to Burke remarkably like Winston Churchill, sat Roberta and Harry Burke down, offered Burke a cigar, was refused, and began to suck on a cheroot himself, looking throughtful. His air of confidence seemed a little forced today. He said with a well-these-things-happen sort of smile that his investigators had come up to the proverbial blank wall.

"You haven't found *any* corroboration of Lorette's story?" cried Roberta.

"None, Miss West."

"But somebody must have seen her somewhere along the line — leaving the building, crossing the park, getting home. . . . It's incredible."

"Unless," said the lawyer, squinting at the tip of his cigar, "she hasn't told us or the police the truth. You know, you can't find what never was."

"I don't think that's the answer at all, Mr. Frankell," Burke said. "I tell you again, that girl is innocent. It's the premise you must go on, or she hasn't a chance."

"Oh, of course," said the lawyer. "I merely raised the possibility; the district attorney is certainly going to more than raise it. What I'm counting on is Lorette's ability to communicate her little-girl quality to the jury. She's the only defense we have."

"You're putting her in the witness box?"

"We call it 'stand' over here, Mr. Burke." Frankell shrugged. "I have no choice. It's always risky, because it opens the defendant up to an all-out attack by the D.A. on cross-examination. I've been over it with Lorette a number of times, playing the devil's advocate, so she'll have a good idea of what she's facing. She stands up well. Of course, how she'll handle herself under actual cross remains to be seen. I warned her —"

His secretary came in, shutting the door behind her.

"Miss Hunter, I told you I wasn't to be interrupted!"

"I'm sorry, Mr. Frankell, but I thought this might be important, and I didn't want to talk over the intercom in front of him —"

"In front of whom?"

"A man just came into the office who insists on seeing you right away. Ordinarily I would have said you're out, but he claims it's about the Spanier case. He's very shabbily dressed. In fact —"

"I don't care if he's in his underwear, Miss Hunter. Send him in!"

162

Even Frankell was startled by the creature his secretary showed in. The man was not shabbily dressed; what he wore was a catastrophe — a ruin of an overcoat which looked as if it had been retrieved from a garbage dump; under it a velveteen smoking jacket of trash-barrel vintage, motheaten, runneled with dregs, spattered with old egg, stewstains, and less identifiable slumgullion; a pair of muddy trousers, evidently cast off by some fat man, held up at the waist by a length of filthy rope; shoes two sizes too big; he wore no socks or shirt. He was skeleton-thin, but his hands and face were puffy, his eyes bloodshot and watering, his nose a purple lump. He had not shaved in days.

He stood before them, shivering as if he had never in his life been warm, and rubbed his palms together. They made a sandpaper sound.

"You asked to see me," Uri Frankell said, staring at him. "Okay, you see me. What's the pitch? Who are you?"

"Name of Spotty," the man said. He had a hoarse, wine-soaked voice. "Name of Spotty," he repeated. He added, with a grin that was almost a leer, "Counselor."

"What do you want?"

"Dough," the derelict said. "Do-re-mi. Lots of it." He stood there grinning; half the teeth in his mouth were missing. "Now ask me what I got to sell, Counselor."

"Look, bum," the lawyer said. "I'm going to give you just ten seconds to spill what's on your

163

mind. And if this is a pitch for a handout, I'll heave you all the way back to the Bowery."

"No, you won't. Not when you hear what I got to sell."

"Well, what?"

"Inf'mation."

"About Lorette Spanier?"

"That's it, Counselor."

"How do you know about Miss Spanier?"

"I read the papers."

"If so, you're the first bum in Bowery history to do it. All right, what's your information?"

"Oh, no," the man said. "I tell you, and what do I get? A boot in the backside is what. On the line, mister."

"Get out of here."

"No, wait," Harry Burke said. He said to the derelict, "You mean you actually expect payment in advance?"

The bleary eyes slid Burke's way. "That's it, mister. And none o' your checks, neither. Cash. On the line."

"How much?" Burke asked.

The purple tip of his tongue appeared. Roberta West watched it, fascinated. It swished across his lips and back, like a rain-wiper.

"A grand."

"A thousand dollars?" the lawyer said incredulously. "You don't want much, do you? What do you think we are, halfwits? Go on, scram."

"Just a moment, Mr. Frankell," the Scot said. "Now see here, Spotty, try being reasonable.

You walk in here and ask for a thousand dollars on your unsupported claim that you have information that may help Miss Spanier's defense. You'll have to admit you're not the most reliable-looking bloke in New York. How can you expect a reputable attorney like Mr. Frankell to pay out so much of his client's money for a blind article?"

"Who are you?" the man demanded.

"A friend of Lorette Spanier's. So is this lady."

"I know about *her* — I seen her picture in the paper. How can I expect, mister? Take it or leave it. Them's my terms. From what the paper says," the bum grinned, "she ain't got much of a case." A scarred thumb wavered Frankell's way.

Probably never before in his derelict life, Burke thought, had this wino been in possession of a highly negotiable asset. And he had the natural cynicism of the downtrodden everywhere. Spotty was not going to be budged. Nevertheless, Burke thought he must try.

He put on his most man-to-man expression.

"Can't you give us at least a hint, Spotty? The sort of information it is?"

"How do I know what sort? I ain't no lawyer."

"But you know enough to know that the information is worth a thousand dollars to Miss Spanier's attorney?"

"All I know is it's about the Spanier dame, and it sounds to me like it's mighty important."

"And if it turns out not to be?"

"That's his hard luck. The grand in advance,

165

and the counselor takes his chances." The bony jaws set. "I ain't giving no money-back guarantee." The jaws set harder.

"Let it drop, Mr. Burke," Frankell said wearily. "I know this breed, believe me. It's probably a sheer invention in the first place. If I paid him for it I'd have to hire Pinkerton guards to keep all the rest of the Bowery bums out of my office, once the word got around. But even if it's legitimate . . . I'll tell you what I'll do with you, Spotty. You tell me what the information is, here and now. If I think it can help Miss Spanier's case, I'll pay you for the information — what I think it's worth. That's the only deal I'll make with you. Taking or leaving?"

They could see in the man's watery eyes the struggle between cupidity and suspicion. They also saw suspicion win.

"No grand, no talk."

He shut his broken mouth with finality.

"Okay, bum, you've spoken your piece. Out."

The derelict stared at the lawyer. Then he grinned again, slyly this time. "You change your mind, Counselor, ask around the Bowery for Spotty. I'll get the word."

He shuffled out.

The moment the door closed Roberta burst out, "But we can't let him go this way. Mr. Frankell! Suppose he's telling the truth — has really important information? Look, if you feel you can't go into a deal like this, I mean as

166

Lorette's lawyer, how about my putting the money up?"

"Do you have a thousand dollars to throw away, Miss West?"

"I'll borrow it — take out a personal loan from my bank —"

"That's up to you," the lawyer said, shrugging. "But believe me, Lorette Spanier isn't going to be acquitted through the sherry-colored imagination of some providential Bowery bum."

Roberta caught the man in the hall as he waited for the elevator. "Wait a second, Mr. Spotty," she panted. Burke was with her, watching the derelict closely. "I'll pay you the money!"

The man put his dirty hand out.

"I don't have that much on me. I'll have to arrange to get it."

"Better arrange fast, lady. That trial starts tomorrow."

"Where can I reach you?"

"I'll reach you, lady. When will you have it?"

"Tomorrow, if I can."

"You going to the trial?"

"Of course —"

"I'll get to you there." He winked at her, a rather elaborate process. He stepped into the elevator and the door closed.

Harry Burke made a dive for the fire door.

"Harry! Where are you going?"

"After him."

"Is that wise? It might get him mad —"

"He won't see me."

167

"Wait! I'll go with you. Does he really know something, do you think?" Roberta panted as they raced down the stairs.

"Frankell's probably right," Harry Burke panted back over his shoulder. "But we can't afford to pass up even a long shot, Bertie, can we?"

TWENTY-SEVEN

They tailed the bum on a zigzag course that staggered downtown. Spotty paused now and then to panhandle a passerby, in an absentminded way — not so much for the dime or quarter, they would have sworn, as to keep his hand in. Below Union Square the man's shuffle quickened. At Cooper Square he bore east around Cooper Union and homed into the Bowery like a pigeon.

His destination was a 25¢-a-night "hotel" with a diseased sign over its pimpled door. Harry Burke took up his stand two doors down, in the boarded-up entrance to an empty store. The gray of the sky began to turn slate; snow was palpable in the raw air. Roberta shivered.

"There's really no point in your sticking this with me," Burke said to her. "This may go on and on."

"But what are you planning to do, Harry?"

"I told you — stick it," he said grimly. "Spotty should come out sooner or later, and when he does I want to see where he goes. There may be others involved."

"Well, if you're going to stay here, Harry Burke, so am I," Roberta said. She began to stamp her tiny feet.

"You're shaking." He pulled her to him in the doorway. She looked up at him. For a moment they were silent. Then Burke flushed and released her.

"I'm not really cold." She was wearing a forest green fuzzy-piled coat with a standup collar. "It's these men, Harry. How can the poor things stand it? Most of them don't even have an overcoat."

"If they had, they'd sell it for the price of a pint of wine or a shot of whisky."

"Are you really as heartless as you sound?"

"Facts are facts," Burke said stubbornly. "Although it's true I'm no bleeding heart. I've seen too much misery no one can do anything about." He said suddenly, "You must be getting hungry, Bertie."

"I'm *starved.*"

"I noticed a cafeteria a block or so north. Why don't you fetch us a few sandwiches like a good girl, and a couple of cartons of coffee? I'd go, but I can't chance Spotty's slipping out in the meanwhile."

"Well . . ." Roberta sounded doubtful. She was eying the passing derelicts.

"Don't worry about the bums. If they accost you, Bertie, tell them you're a policewoman. You're safer among men like these than you would be uptown. Sex isn't their problem. Here." Burke pressed a $5 bill on her.

"I can pay for it. Goodness!"

"I'm old-fashioned." To Burke's astonish-

170

ment, he found himself smacking her round little bottom. She looked startled, but she did not seem to mind. "On your way, wench!"

She was gone fifteen minutes.

"Any trouble?"

"One man stopped me. When he heard the magic word he almost sprained an ankle getting away."

Burke grinned and uncapped the coffee.

Darkness fell. The scarred flophouse door began to do a brisk business. There was no sign of the man who called himself Spotty.

It began to snow.

Two hours dragged by. It was now snowing heavily. Burke, too, stamped his feet.

"I don't understand it . . ."

"He must have gone to bed."

"While it was still daylight?"

"I don't see what we're accomplishing here, Harry," Roberta complained. "Except risking pneumonia."

"There's something wrong," Burke muttered.

"Wrong? How do you mean?"

"I don't know. Except that it makes no sense, his going in before dark and remaining there. He'd have to eat, and there's certainly no dining room in that black hole." Burke seemed suddenly to make up his mind about something. "Roberta."

"Yes, Harry?"

"I'm sending you home." He seized her arm and steered her across the sidewalk to the curb.

"But why? I mean, aren't you going, too?"

"I'm going into that fleatrap, which you obviously can't do. And even if you could, I wouldn't allow you to. And I'd rather not leave you standing out here alone."

He shook off Roberta's protests, managed to commandeer a taxi, and packed her into it. She craned back at him rather forlornly as the cab took off, its chains slapping and clanking and spitting slush. But Harry Burke was already hurrying toward the bums' hotel.

TWENTY-EIGHT

The lobby proved to be a small, poorly varnished desk at the end of a dark hallway, presided over by an old man with a blue-veined nose and acne. The old man wore a heavy sweater; the rusty radiator was hissing, but the place was like the grave. The only illumination came from a 60-watt bulb dangling over the desk under a scratched green glass shade. There was a staircase at one side, with a railing. The steps were worn down in the middle, and the railing reflected a sickish gloss in the murk.

"I'm looking for a man who checked in just before nightfall," Burke said to the old man. "He calls himself Spotty."

"Spotty?" The old man stared suspiciously. "What you want Spotty for?"

"Which room is he in?"

"You a cop?" When Burke said nothing, the old man said, "What's Spotty done?" He had dark brown teeth.

Burke's tone hardened. "Which room is he in?"

"Okay, mister, keep your benny on. We got no private rooms here. Dorms. He's in Dorm A."

"Where is that?"

"Up the stairs and to your right."

"You come with me."

"I got to stay at the desk —"

"Old man, you're wasting my time."

The old man grumbled. But he came out from behind his desk and led the way up the stairs.

Dorm A was like something out of the *Inferno*. It was a long narrow room with cramped ranks of cots on each side, a filthy and cracked linoleum floor that looked like a relief map and a naked red bulb hanging from a cord in the middle of the ceiling which bathed the scene in blood. Half the thirty cots were already occupied. The room was unpleasantly alive — snuffles, mutters, snores, thrashings about; a blended stench of unwashed bodies, dirty clothing, urine, and alcohol fumes. There was no heat, and the two windows at the end of the room looked as if they had not been opened in a century.

"Which bed is he in?" Burke demanded of the old man.

"How in hell should I know? First come, first served."

He went up one side, followed by the old man. Burke stooped over each cot. The dim red light made his eyes water. He found himself holding his breath.

The man called Spotty lay on the other side of the room on the rearmost cot. He had his face to the wall, and he was covered to the neck by the blanket.

"That's him," the old man said. He pushed

past Burke and punched the still shoulder. "Spotty! Wake the hell up!"

Spotty failed to stir.

"Must of had a bottle," the old man said. He jerked the blanket off. He fell back, all his brown teeth showing.

The handle of a switchblade stuck out of the derelict's overcoated back, on the left side. The only blood Burke could see looked black in the red light. He felt for the carotid artery.

He straightened up. "Do you have a telephone?" he asked the old man.

"He dead?"

"Yes."

The old man cursed. "Downstairs," he said.

"Don't touch anything, and don't wake the other men up —"

Burke went downstairs.

TWENTY-NINE

Inspector Queen's interrogation took until 3:00 A.M. Twice Burke and Ellery walked over to the allnight cafeteria for coffee; the cold in the flophouse went in to the bone.

"He had something," Burke muttered. "He really did. I knew it. But that damned Frankell had to freeze him out."

"You didn't recognize anyone going into the place, Harry?" Ellery asked him.

"I was concentrating on spotting Spotty, damn it all."

"Too bad."

"Don't rub it in. I'm trying to tell myself that the knifer may have got in and out through the rear. There's a rear door, off an alley, and a back stairs."

Ellery nodded and sipped his coffee, which was horrible but hot. He said no more. Burke seemed to be taking the murder of the derelict personally; for that disease there was no remedy.

"We'll get nothing here," the Inspector said when he had finished upstairs. "The knife is a cheap switchblade, and there are no prints on it. And if these bums know anything, they're not opening their traps."

"Then why are we hanging around here?" Ellery complained. "I can think of better places to be. My sweet clean bed, for instance."

"One thing," his father said. "While you and Burke were out I questioned a man who claims this Spotty had a pal, somebody they call Mugger. The two seem to have been thick as the thieves they are — or at least Mugger is. He got his monicker for good and sufficient reason, Velie tells me."

"Mugging record long as your arm," Sergeant Velie said. "Works the quiet dark spots. Never hurts anybody, far as we know. He likes to pick on the soft touches — old people mostly."

"Have you talked to the man yet?" Burke asked.

"He's not here," the Inspector replied. "That's why I'm waiting. In case he shows up."

The man reeled in at 3:30 A.M., decks awash. It took three cartons of black coffee to heave him to within reasonable sight of sobriety. After that, when Sergeant Velie told him with calculated callousness that his pal Spotty had gone out the hard way, with a shiv in his back, Mugger began to blubber. It was a fascinating sight. He was a wrecked fat brute of a man who looked as if he might once have been a heavyweight prize-fighter. He would say absolutely nothing to all questions.

But he underwent a sea change when they drove him up to the Morgue and showed him his friend's body.

"Okay," he growled, *"okay,"* and spat on the floor, hard.

They found him a chair. He overflowed it, glowering at the aseptic walls.

"You going to talk now?" Inspector Queen asked him.

"Depends."

"On what?"

"On what you ask." It was evident that any question involving his nocturnal activities would be out of the answering zone.

"All right," said the Inspector. "Let's try this on for size: You knew what Spotty had to sell, didn't you?"

"Info on that girl up for trial tomorrow on the murder rap."

"You were partners with Spotty? Going to split the take?"

"Spotty didn't know I knew."

"What was the information?"

The man was silent. His bloody eyes roved, as if seeking safe harbor.

"Look, Mugger," the Inspector said. "You may be pretty deep in these woods. Spotty knew something he said would help Miss Spanier. And he was going to collect a thousand dollars for it. You knew what it was all about. That gives you a mighty good motive to want Spotty out of the scene. If Spotty was dead, you could take over and collect the thousand for your own self. Looks as if we're going to have to trace that switchblade to you."

178

"Me? Shiv Spotty?" Life crept into the devastated eyes. "My buddy?"

"Don't hand me that buddy stuff. There's no such thing as a buddy on your beat. Not where a score is concerned."

"He was," Mugger said earnestly. "Ask anybody."

"I'm telling you. You either stuck that blade into him — and if you did we'll nail you for it — or you were waiting for Spotty to make the score and then you'd step in. It's one or the other. Which?"

Mugger ran the back of his hairy hand across his mashed nose. He looked around and saw nothing but hostile eyes. He sighed deeply. "Okay," he said, "so I was going to let Spotty do it. Then I'd put in for my half. Spotty would split with me. We was pals. I kid you not."

"What was the information Spotty was trying to sell?" Inspector Queen asked again.

It was almost 6:00 A.M. before the man could bring himself to reveal the precious information. And then it was only when Sergeant Velie brought out some precious information of his own. Mugger was a parolee on a mugging rap. One word to his parole officer about his uncooperative attitude, and he would find himself back in the can. Or so Velie alleged. Mugger was not disposed to argue the point. He spilled.

As a matter of routine, the sergeant checked him out for the Spotty killing. He was clean. He had an alibi attested by two bartenders in a Bow-

179

ery joint. He had not left the bar from midafter-
noon until past midnight (and what he had been
doing between past midnight and 3:30 A.M. they
could guess, which was not difficult, considering
the vocation that had earned him his monicker).

The alibi that stood up strengthened his story
about Lorette Spanier, although Inspector Queen
pointed out that a defense based upon the testimony of a witness of Mugger's nature and
character was hardly the sort of thing defense at-
torneys greeted with huzzahs.

The last thing they did in that dawn was to
spirit the hulk to an out-of-the-way hotel, where
they locked him in under police guard.

As Ellery said, "Whoever killed Spotty has the
identical hex against Mugger. Let's keep him
alive at least until he can testify."

He and Harry Burke went their respective ways
for a few hours' sleep. Ellery found Morpheus
slippery. He thought, as he rotated on his axis in
bed, that he now saw half the face of the mystery
as it rotated on *its* axis. But if the three-quarter
face was coming round into focus, it was taking
its sweet time.

3   THREE-QUARTER FACE

The countenance is the portrait of the mind, the eyes are its informers.

CICERO

THIRTY

For a man who had been so cavalierly confident that he could cast doubt on the People's case against his client, Uri Frankell, seized the straw handed him by the unexpected defense witness with remarkable alacrity.

"I naturally prefer positive to negative testimony," the defense attorney said, "in a trial by jury."

"Why don't you try to get the D.A. to withdraw the charge?" Ellery asked him. "Then you won't have to go to a jury at all."

"Herman wouldn't buy it," Frankell said. "Not with this character as my witness. In fact, that's what we've got chiefly to worry about. He's going to light into Mugger like a bum into a Salvation Army turkey."

"Then do you think it wise to restrict the menu to the turkey?"

"It's the best we've got."

"I thought you were relying on Lorette. Have you changed your mind about putting her on the stand?"

"We'll see. It all depends on how it goes with Mugger." Frankell looked cautious. "You're sure he wasn't offered a consideration for his testimony? No promise of or actual money payment — anything like that?"

"I'm sure."

"Then why is he so willing to testify? I couldn't get it out of him."

"It was tactfully suggested to him in the original police interrogation that he might wind up back in prison if he was uncooperative. He's a parolee."

"This was a police threat? Not made by someone on our side?"

"That's right."

Frankell looked glad.

The district attorney did his usual workmanlike job without, Ellery noted, his usual *joie d'oeuvrer*. It was not so much the nature of Herman's case, Ellery decided, as the nature of his witnesses. With the exception of officials, like Inspector Queen and Sergeant Velie, those who had to testify to the circumstances were hostile to his case or, at the least, sympathetic to the defendant. Carlos Armando, Harry Burke, Roberta West, Ellery himself, had had to be subpoenaed. They were far more compliant under cross-examination than direct questioning.

Nevertheless, by the time the People rested, the district attorney had blocked out a persuasive case against Lorette Spanier. She was the last person known to have been alone with Glory Guild before the singer's death. Her statement as to the time of her departure from the Guild apartment, her homeward walk across Central

Park, and her arrival at her flat was without support of any kind. The .38 Special that had taken Glory's life had been found in the defendant's closet, in a hatbox belonging to her. She was the victim's principal heir to a considerable estate. She had been neglected — the D.A. used the word "abandoned" — by the victim since early childhood, implying that the motive had been either gain or hatred, or both.

The jury seemed impressed. Their multiple eye persistently avoided the blond child-face at the defense table.

Frankell opened and closed his case with Mugger. It was a far different Mugger from the derelict Lorette's friends had last seen. His suit had been dry-cleaned and pressed; he was wearing a clean white shirt, a dark necktie, and a pair of shined shoes; he was blue-shaven; and he was cold if bleary-eyed sober. He looked amazingly like a hardworked plumber dressed for church. ("Sure Herman will bring out that we prettied him up," the defense lawyer murmured to Ellery. "But it's going to take a lot of hammering away to make the jury forget how decent the guy looks. Personally, I think we've got Herman hung up. What's more, Herman knows it. Look at his nose." The district attorney's nostrils were shuttling in and out as if searching for bad odors which, for all their experience, they could not detect.)

It turned out that Mugger's name was a surprising Curtis Perry Hathaway. Frankell promptly elicited from Mr. Hathaway the information that he was "sometimes" known as Mugger. ("Why did you ask that?" Ellery demanded later. "Because," the lawyer replied, "Herman would if I didn't. Took the sting out of it. Or the stink — take your choice.")

"How did you get your nickname, Mr. Hathaway?"

"I broke my nose playing baseball when I was a kid," Mugger said earnestly. "It give me this ugly mug, see, which I would make faces — you know, clown around, the way kids do — because I was ashamed. So they begin to call me Mugger." ("Oh, my ears and whiskers," muttered Harry Burke.)

"Now, Mr. Hathaway," said Uri Frankell, "you're under oath, a witness for the defendant, an important witness, I might say the most important witness, and we've got to be dead certain the Court and the jury understand just who you are and how you stand in all this, so that nobody can come along later and say we tried to conceal something —"

"He means me!" yelled the district attorney. "I object to speeches!"

"Mr. Frankell, do you have another question of this witness?"

"Lots of them, your Honor."

"Then ask them, will you?"

"Mr. Hathaway, you have just told us how you came to get the nickname Mugger. Is there any other reason?"

"For what?"

"For your being called Mugger."

"No, *sir*," said Mugger.

"Mr. Hathaway —" began Frankell.

"Leading the witness!" shouted the district attorney.

"I fail to see how pronouncing the witness's name is leading him," said his Honor. "Go ahead, Mr. Frankell. But don't lead him."

"Mr. Hathway, do you have a police record?"

Mugger looked crushed. "What kind of a question is that, for gossakes?"

"Never mind what kind it is. Answer it."

"I been pulled in a few times." Mugger's tone said, Isn't everybody?

"On what charge?"

"Mugging, they put it down. Listen, I never mugged nobody in my whole life. You mug, you hurt people. I don't hurt people. Never. Only they tag you with it, it sticks —"

"The witness will answer the question and stop," his Honor said. "Mr. Frankell, I don't want speeches from your witnesses, either."

"Just answer my question, Mr. Hathaway, and stop."

"But they tagged me —"

"Isn't that also why you're sometimes called Mugger, Mr. Hathaway? Because the police collared you on a few alleged mugging raps?"

"I told you. They tagged me —"

"All right, Mr. Hathaway, we understand. But the principal reason you're called Mugger is that you've borne the nickname from childhood because of your nose being broken playing baseball and you clowned about it, made funny faces?"

"Yes, *sir.*"

"I was under the impression that this witness was testifying for the defendant," his Honor remarked to Uri Frankell, "not for himself. Will you please get with it?"

"Yes, your Honor, but we don't wish to conceal anything from the Court and the jury —"

"No speeches, Counselor!"

"Yes, sir. Now, Mr. Hathaway, did you know a man named John Tumelty?"

"Who?" said Mugger.

"Better known as Spotty."

"Oh, Spotty. Sure. He was my pal. Real buddies, we was."

"Where is your pal Spotty now?"

"In the cooler."

"You mean in the city Morgue?"

"That's what I said. Somebody cooled him good the other night. Stuck a shiv in his back while he was grabbing some shuteye." Mugger sounded indignant. It was as if he would have felt better about his friend had Spotty come to an end on the *qui vive* and face to face with the author who was about to write finis to his life.

"Is that why Spotty isn't here today testifying for Miss Spanier?"

"Object!" cried the district attorney, flapping his fat hand.

"Of course," said his Honor nastily. "You know better than that, Mr. Frankell. Strike the

188

question. The jury will disregard it." Mugger opened his mouth. "Witness, don't you answer!" Mugger shut his mouth. "Proceed, Counselor."

"Before we get to the meat of your testimony, Mr. Hathaway," Frankell said, "I wish to clear up something for these good ladies and gentlemen of the jury. I ask you — and remember you're under oath — have you been offered any money or other material consideration for your testimony in this case?"

"Not one dime," said Mugger, not without bitterness.

"You're sure of that?"

"Sure I'm sure."

"Not by the defendant?"

"The who?"

"The lady on trial."

"No, sir."

"Not by me?"

"You? No, sir."

"Not by any of Miss Spanier's friends?"

"Not me."

"Not by —"

"How many times does he have to answer the same question?" inquired the D.A.

"— by anyone connected with the defense?"

"I told you. Not by nobody."

"Then why are you testifying, Mr. Hathaway?"

"The fuzz," said Mugger.

"The fuzz?"

"The fuzz told me if I didn't answer their

questions on the up and up they'd tell my parole officer."

"Oh. The police told you that when they were interrogating you? When was that?"

"The night they found Spotty shivved."

"So it's because of police pressure that you're giving your testimony — your truthful testimony — in this case?"

"Object!" howled the district attorney. "Unwarranted inference! The next thing we'll hear is about police brutality in a routine interrogation!"

"Take your seat, Mr. District Attorney," sighed his Honor. "Mr. Frankell, phrase your questions in the proper way. I'm getting tired of telling you. There has been no testimony adduced from this witness as to police pressure."

"I'm sorry, your Honor," said Uri Frankell in a sorry voice. "The point is that this witness's testimony is the result of a police grilling, not from any offer of consideration to the witness by the defense —"

"And don't use the word grilling, Mr. Frankell! Get on, get on!"

"Yes, your Honor. Now, Mr. Hathaway, I want to take you back to certain events that occurred on the night of Wednesday, December the thirtieth last."

There was an immediate and sensible tightening in the courtroom. It was as if everyone present — in the jury box, among the spectators, in the press section — was telling himself, Here it comes! without knowing just what was on the way, but anticipating, from Frankell's buildup, that it was going to be a real swinger of a blow to the poor public servant at the prosecution table. Even his Honor leaned forward. Among the certain events that had occurred on the night of Wednesday, December the thirtieth last, was GeeGee Guild's push toward eternity.

"Do you recall that night, Mr. Hathaway?"

"I do, " said Mugger, as fervently as if he were at the altar.

"That's quite a while ago. What makes you remember that particular night after all this time?"

" 'Cause I hit a real score," said Mugger, licking his blasted lips at the recollection. "Nothing like that ever happened to me before. That was some night."

"And what was the unusual event on that memorable night, Mr. Hathaway?"

Mr. Hathaway hesitated, lips moving silently in communion with the glorious past.

"Come, come, Mr. Hathaway, we're waiting," said Frankell in an indulgent way. His eyes were saying, Stop looking as if you're rehearsing your testimony, damn you.

"Oh! Yeah," said Mr. Hathaway. "Well, it's like this, see. It's a cold night, and I'm kind of short. So I goes up to this guy and asks can he help me out. Sure, my man, he says to me. And he pulls out his leather and smooches around in it and finally comes up with a bill and sticks it in my hand. I take a look and almost drop dead. It's a fifty. Fifty bucks! While I'm still wondering am I dreaming he says, ' 'Tis the season to be merry, old friend. But never let us forget that it's later than we think. Here, you take this, too.' And he pulls off his wristwatch and gives me *that*. 'Every man,' he says to me, 'is got to keep an eye on the rear end of Father Time,' or something like that — and off he staggers before I can say a word."

"Staggers? You mean he was intoxicated?" asked Frankell quickly, not looking at the jury.

"I don't mean he was sober," said Mugger. "Higher'n the Empire State Building. Full o' sauce. Nice joe. Nicest I ever met." Ellery would not have been surprised had Mugger added, "God bless him."

"Where did this encounter take place?"

"On Forty-third off Eighth."

This time Frankell did look at the jury. Ellery could only admire his astuteness. Frankell knew that no man or woman in the courtroom believed Mugger's yarn about the manner in which he had come by his windfall. Each mind was thinking, He rolled the poor shnook. Sheer technique demanded a frontal attack on the implausibility of the story.

"Let us get this straight. You say you approached a drunk in the Times Square district and asked him for a handout, and he promptly and voluntarily gave you a fifty-dollar bill and his wristwatch?"

"I don't expect nobody to believe me," said Mugger simply. "I couldn't hardly believe it myself. But that's just what he done, so help me. And I never laid a finger on him."

"And this occurred on the night before New Year's Eve?" Frankell asked hurriedly.

"Yeah. He must have got a head start on the bottle."

The jury was hooked. There had been an astonishment in Mugger's voice, an afterglow of wonder at his incredible luck, that could only recall Cinderella's feelings at the touch of the Fairy Godmother's wand. Frankell was satisfied. He pressed on.

"All right, then. What happened?"

"What happened? Nothing. I mean I had to tell somebody about it — Spotty. I couldn't wait to tell Spotty. So I went on up to Central Park —"

"Why Central Park?"

"That's where Spotty liked to make his scores. I figure I'll find him working his old territory, so I go on up there and sure enough I find him."

"Let's take this step by step, Mr. Hathaway. You could hardly wait to tell your pal John Tumelty, or Spotty as you call him, about your good fortune, so you went to the place where he usually operated, in Central Park, and you did find him. Did you speak to him the moment you found him?"

"How could I? I come up the walk and I spot him stopping this young broad — lady. So I wait behind a bush till he's through."

"He was begging a handout from a young lady. Do you see that young lady, Mr. Hatha-

193

way, in this courtroom?"

"Sure I do."

"Oh, you do? Would you point her out to us, please?"

Mugger's cleansed forefinger pointed smack at Lorette Spanier.

"Let the record show," said Frankell briskly, "that the witness indicated Miss Lorette Spanier, the defendant." He was all confidence now. "Now I want you to pay close attention, Mr. Hathaway, and be very sure you answer with the exact truth. Did you, at the time you were in the bushes while Spotty was talking to Miss Spanier in Central Park — did you have occasion to glance at the watch the intoxicated man had given you?"

"You betcha."

"Why did you look at the watch?"

"Why did I look at it? Say, I'd been looking at it all the way uptown to the park. I hadn't had a watch for so long I couldn't hardly believe I wasn't dreaming."

"So when you looked at the watch while your pal Spotty was accosting Miss Spanier, you were doing so simply because of the novelty of it? The novelty of having a watch to look at after so many years?"

"You could say that," said Mugger, nodding. "Yeah, that's it, all right. The novelty."

"By the way, do you happen to know if the watch was set accurately?"

"Come again?"

"Was the watch telling the right time?"

"Was it! I checked it against the street clocks and the clocks in stores must have been a dozen times on my way up. What's the good having a watch if it don't give you the right time?"

"No good at all, Mr. Hathaway, I agree absolutely. So your watch was set to the right time, according to a dozen clocks you consulted on your walk uptown." Frankell asked casually, "And what time did your watch tell you it was when you saw Spotty stop Miss Spanier for a handout."

Mugger said promptly, "Twenty minutes to twelve on the schnozz."

"Twenty minutes to twelve on the schnozz. You're sure of that, Mr. Hathaway?"

"Sure I'm sure. Ain't I just got through telling you? Twenty minutes to twelve."

"This was twenty minutes to midnight?"

"I just said it."

"On the night of Wednesday, December thirtieth last, the night before New Year's Eve — the night Glory Guild was murdered?"

"Yes, sir."

"In Central Park?"

"*In* Central Park."

Frankell turned and began to walk back toward the defense table. The expression on the district attorney's face seemed to stir his sympathy. He smiled sadly in the D.A.'s direction, as if to say, Sorry, old man, *mais c'est la guerre, n'est-ce pas?* But then he suddenly turned back to Mugger.

"Oh, one thing more. Did Miss Spanier — the young lady sitting over there — did she give Spotty anything after his pitch?"

"Yeah. After she walked away and I stepped out of the bushes and went over to Spotty, he showed me the quarter she give him, like it was a bonanza." Mugger shook his head. "Poor old Spots. A lousy — a measly quarter, and me with half a C note in my jeans. I almost didn't have the heart to show it to him."

"Did you happen to notice in which direction Miss Spanier walked after she left Spotty?"

"Sure, she walked west. It was on the cross-town walk, so she had to be headed for the West Side exit."

"Thank *you*, Mr. Hathaway," said Frankell tenderly. "Your witness," he waved to the district attorney. Who rose from his chair slightly stooped over, as if he had a bellyache.

THIRTY-ONE

In the innocent orgy celebrating Lorette's acquittal, there was unanimous agreement that she was indeed the child of fortune. How she had come to forget about the derelict who had accosted her during her walk across the Park after leaving her aunt she could not say; it had simply left no impression on her. As Ellery reminded her, if it had not been for an openhanded drunk, a thunderstruck mugger, and a panhandling wino, Lorette would probably have wound up on the unpleasant side of the verdict. (He did not remind her that someone had permanently stopped the mouth of the wino to keep it from wagging in just such a courtroom — the same someone who had planted the Colt Detective in her Saks box. After all, it was a celebration.)

Even Curtis Perry Hathaway, who was included at Lorette's insistent invitation, and who was drinking Irish whisky with both hands, seemed affected. He still bore the scars of his cross-examination at the hands of the district attorney, who had swung wildly from both hips. But Mr. Hathaway had not yielded an inch; Horatius, Harry Burke had dubbed him. Mugger's pockets were full of newspaper clippings attesting to his importance; he looked exhausted, dazzled, full of the milk of *simpático* as well as Duggan's Dew, and totally unbelieving. It was the supreme moment of his life.

Too, now that she was forever free of the charge of murder, cracks had become visible in Lorette's British armor. She was laughing immoderately, chattering away with everyone within earshot; but her unplucked brows were drawn together as if she were in pain, or seeing badly, her blue eyes were mere slits, as if the light hurt them, and the cups of her nostrils looked like unglazed china. It would take very little, Ellery thought, to break her down and start those amazing eyes flowing. At the same time there was a new hardness about her mouth. The childish pout was gone. Instant maturity, he thought. She had gone into this an adolescent and come out of it a woman. And he sighed.

"You look as if you've swallowed a bad oyster," Harry Burke remarked to him a little later. "What's the trouble, chum?"

"Face," Ellery grumbled.

"Whose?" asked Burke, looking around.

"I don't know, Harry. *That's* the trouble."

"Oh."

Whose face had GeeGee Guild meant?

THIRTY-TWO

"Something's the matter," Burke said to her.

"It's nothing, Harry," Roberta said. "Really."

"You can't fool me, duck. Not any more. It's Lorette, isn't it?"

"Well . . ."

"You ought to slow up a bit, Bert. On the Armando business, I mean. You can't keep mothering her. Seems dangerously near resenting it."

"Oh, Harry, I don't want to talk about it! The whole thing has me on the verge of throwing up. Please. Put your arms around me."

Lorette had diplomatically gone to bed — at least she had retired to her bedroom — and they were alone in the cathedral vastness of the penthouse living room.

With Roberta in his arms, Burke closed his eyes. She felt so warm and *right*. The whole world had a rightness these days that not even the periodic sight on the premises of Carlos Armando's dark, pitted face could upset. Why had he wasted all these bachelor years?

Roberta settled herself more deeply into his arms, snuggling like a tired child.

"Harry, I didn't know a man could feel so good,"

she murmured. "I'm so downright grateful."

"Grateful?"

"It's the only word. I wish . . ."

"Yes, Bertie?"

"Nothing."

"You can't begin a sentence like that and leave it dangling! Wish what?"

"Oh, that you'd come along years ago, if you must know."

"You do, luvvie?"

"I wouldn't say it if I didn't mean it. You make me feel — I don't know — the way a woman ought to feel, I suppose. Not . . ."

"Not what?"

"Never mind."

"The way Armando made you feel when you were in love with him?"

She sat up then, fiercely pushing him away. "Don't ever say that to me again, Harry Burke. Ever! I was a ninny. Worse than a ninny. I look back on it now and it seems as if it happened to somebody else. All of it. It did happen to somebody else. I'm not the same person I was then." Her voice trembled. "And you've made the difference, Harry. Don't — see how shameless I am! — don't ever stop making the difference."

"I won't," Burke said, softly; and this time when they kissed there was no nonsense about lust feelings or lips surprised into tenderness. It was the kiss of rightness, ordained by the nature of things, and Burke knew he was hooked. They were both hooked. And it was marvelous.

THIRTY-THREE

"Then it is serious," Ellery said a few days later.

Burke arched his sandy brows across the luncheon table.

"You and Roberta West."

The Scotsman looked uncomfortable. "You do keep after a man. What's your line of reasoning this time?"

"Your last excuse for not winging home was that you felt a responsibility for Lorette Spanier. Lorette's out of the woods, and you linger. If it isn't Lorette, it has to be little Robby. Does she know it yet? How long does a thing like this take you Scots?"

"We're a canny tribe," Burke said, pink-cheeked. "A generally monogamous breed. That sort of thing takes time. Yes, it's serious, chappie, and be damned to you."

"Does Roberta know it yet?"

"I think she does."

"You think! What do you two talk about, anyway."

"There are some things, Horatio, that are simply none of your affair." Burke seemed anxious to change the subject. "Anything new on the case?"

"Nothing."

"Then you've abandoned ship?"

"The hell you say. That face business haunts my bed. By the way, what's this I hear about Lorette and Carlos Armando?" The gossip columns were ripe with hints, and Ellery had not seen Lorette since the night of the celebration.

"It's incredible," Burke said angrily. "The bugger has the gall of a brass monkey, or do I have it mixed up? Women mystify me. You'd think Lorette would see through him. She's a practical girl! But apparently she's as helpless as the rest of the geese when he turns on the charm."

"You have to be born with it," Ellery said. "Well, I'm sorry to hear it. Armando's record should speak for itself."

"To you and me and the rest of male humanity," Burke snapped. "To these women it's a foreign language."

"No way to disillusion her?"

"God knows Roberta's trying. As a matter of fact," and the Scotsman banged the dottle from his pipe, "it's beginning to come between the girls. I've tried to get Bert to take it a bit easy, but Armando is a thing with her. She detests him, and she can't bear to see Lorette getting involved."

Ellery heard from Burke about the blowup between Lorette and Roberta West the following week. Their fight over Armando had reached the moment of truth.

"Look, darling," Roberta had said. "It *is* none of my business, but I can't stand seeing you

202

sucked in by that — that human quicksand."

"Roberta," Lorette had said, chin up. "I'd rather not discuss Carlos with you any more."

"But someone has to pound some sense into you! Letting him send you flowers, date you, hang around here till all hours — don't you realize what you're getting yourself into?"

"Roberta —"

"No, I'm going to say it. Lorette, you're being silly. You've no experience of men, and Carlos's got pelts like yours hanging on his belt by the dozen. He isn't even being clever about it with you. Can't you see that all he wants is the money he didn't get after he married your Aunt Glory?"

Lorette's temper had surged in like surf. But she had made an effort, and half turned away, clenching her little hands. "And can't you stop trying to run my life?"

"But I'm *not,* darling. I'm only trying to keep you out of the clutches of one of the world's ace heels. Who happens to be a murderer, besides."

"Carlos murdered no one!"

"He masterminded it, Lorette. He's guiltier than she is. Whoever she is."

"I don't believe it!"

"Do you think I'd lie about it?"

"Perhaps you would!"

"Why should I? I've told you over and over how Carlos tried to get me to do it for him —"

Lorette had faced her then, her perky nose the color of pearl. "Roberta, I've changed my mind about you. I didn't believe you were that sort, but now I see that you are. You envy me. You're eaten up with it."

"Me? Envious of you?"

"Of the money Aunt Glory left me. And of Carlos's interest in me!"

"You're out of your everloving mind, darling. I'm glad about your good luck. And, as for Carlos's attentions, I'd rather be chased by a shark; I'd be a lot safer. And so would you."

"You *admitted* you were gone on him —"

"That was before I found out what he is. Anyway, that horrible chapter in my life is finished, thank God. If you must know, Lorette, I'm in love with Harry Burke, and I'm sure Harry's in love with me. I couldn't care less about that hand-slobbering monster —"

"That's enough, Roberta." Lorette was shaking. "If you can't keep from slandering Carlos . . ."

She stopped.

"You were going to say that you want me to leave, weren't you?" Roberta asked quietly.

"I said if you can't keep —"

"I know what you said, Lorette. I'll move out the minute I can find a place. Unless you'd rather I did it today — right now?"

The two girls had glared at each other. Finally Lorette had said in her chilliest British voice, "It isn't necessary to do it today. But, under the circumstances, I do think it would be better if we broke off this arrangement as soon as convenient."

204

"I'll be out of here by tomorrow morning."

And Roberta was. She moved into a Y, and Harry Burke helped her find an apartment. It was a dark one and-a-half roomer on York Avenue, in a rundown building, with bars on the street-level window and a bathroom washbowl that had half its procelain chipped off and a crack through which the water dripped. There was a bar on the corner of the block from which men reeled at all hours.

"It's a stinking hole, Bertie," Burke said crossly. "I can't imagine why you took it. If you'd listen to reason —"

"You mean take money from you?"

"Well, what's wrong with that?"

"Everything, Harry, although you're a dear to offer it."

He looked helpless and furious.

"It's not so bad," Roberta said softly, "and at least it's furnished. Anyway, I can't afford anything better. And I'd much rather live here than in Lorette's penthouse watching that animal pull her down with him."

"But it's a rough neighborhood!"

"Lorette's place," said Roberta, "is loads rougher."

So she moved in with her few belongings, and Harry Burke became her private security guard. He may have made his self-appointment harder than the job actually was — there were plenty of other people living in the building who could not afford higher rents, and they seemed to survive the hazards of the neighborhood — but one night Burke collared a dish-haired youth in a shiny black jacket and jackboots as the boy crouched at Roberta's window, peeping hotly through the bars and the crack in the drapes at the undressing girl. The Scot did not call the police. He took the boy's switchblade away, kicked him in the tail, and warned him as he fled that the building was off limits to beats, kooks, deviates, perverts in all classifications, and just plain mischief-hunters, and to be sure to tell his friends. After that, Burke felt better. He even fixed the unreliable front-door lock at his own expense, saying to Roberta, "That ought to kill the myth that Scots are tight with their money." Roberta kissed him rather more warmly than his 49¢ expenditure warranted; so he bought heaven for three and six, which even in Scotland would have been held a bargain.

THIRTY-FOUR

What happened to Lorette was an old story to Ellery who was native-born and steeped in the American juices; to alien Burke, such Anglicisms as the Profumo case notwithstanding, it was an astonishment. The heroine of the liberating courtroom, following cultural precedent, became an overnight celebrity, with all the appurtenances thereto appertaining, including a contract.

"Only ignorance accounts for your surprise, Harry," Ellery said kindly. "Over here we reward homicide as a matter of national course. We dote on our murderers. Photograph them, interview them, beg them for autographs, raise funds for their defense, fight for a glimpse of them, and burst into tears when they're acquitted. Some of us even marry them. I understand that Truman Capote has been spending his past few years — years, mind you — picking away at a particularly senseless Kansas massacre, just to get a book out of it. Just? He'll sell millions."

"But to sign her for Broadway!" Burke protested.

"Of course. You're simply not with it, Harry. These days in the U.S.A. civil rights means something. Why should a WASP of the tender sex be discriminated against because my father and the D.A. thought she'd murdered her aunt? Although I understand Lorette's case doesn't altogether conform to the democratic ideal. She's supposed to have talent."

"So has Roberta," the Scot said bitterly. "But I don't see anyone offering her a contract."

"Tell Roberta to go out and get accused of shooting somebody."

Lorette had been bombarded with so many offers — TV appearances, nightclub work, even a motion picture contract — that, at Uncle Carlos's tactical suggestion, she had turned to Selma Pilter for guidance. The old veteran of the percentage wars, whose affection for Lorette dated from that day in William Maloney Wasser's office, charged into the battle. It was she who captured the Broadway contract.

"But Selma," Lorette said nervously, "Broadway . . ."

"Look, my dear," Selma Pilter said. "If you're serious about a singing career, there's no quicker way to recognition. I don't see you kicking around the clubs for years. If you're going to become a star you've got to command a star's audience. And, while television is good exposure, it's no shortcut. Look at Barbra Streisand — it wasn't until she hit Broadway that she made it big. GeeGee climbed to the top on radio, but that was a different era. You've had the publicity, now you need the vehicle. And right away, while the public still remembers you. That's why I ad-

208

vised you to turn down the Hollywood offer — Hollywood takes too long. Of course, if you didn't have star quality, it would be another story. But with your voice, on top of what's just happened to you, you can't miss."

"Do you really think so?"

"I'm too old in this game to waste my time on mediocrity. So, I might add, is Orrin Steyne. If Orrin wants you for his musical, he thinks you'll make it. He's not going to risk nearly half a million dollars of his backers' money, let alone his reputation, on a mere pretty face and a few dozen yards of news clippings."

"Will I be playing the lead?"

The old woman grinned. "You're talking like a star already. Dear, this is a musical revue. Loaded with fresh young talent — Orrin's a master at picking tomorrow's stars. What he has in mind for you is a single — just you, a piano, and a spotlight. He couldn't show more confidence in you. My advice is to take it."

Lorette took it and the buildup began. Between Selma Pilter and Steyne's press agent, not to mention the likes of Kip Kipley, she received the full treatment. Quietly, Marta Bellina, back from her tour, gave the girl lessons in breathing and projection. "It's the least I can do for Glory's niece," the aging opera singer told her. "And your voice does so remind me of hers."

Ellery, still fitfully chasing the four-letter will-o'-the-wisp in the Guild murder, took time off to satisfy himself on that score. He cabbed over to the doddering Roman Theater on West 47th Street, where Steyne's company was rehearsing, and with the help of a nodding acquaintance with the doorman and a five-spot, slipped into one of the last-row seats for a personal audition.

It was true. The resemblance raised goose pimples. The girl was a natural instrumentalist of the voice — the same voice, Ellery would have sworn, that came out of the ancient Glory Guild records he cherished.

Lorette sat at the grand on the naked stage, in street clothes, without makeup, a frowning preoccupation on her little face as she occasionally squinted at the lyrics on the sheets. From her throat came the same faint throb that had bewitched her aunt's radio millions. Like the intimate Guild voice, it drew its audience close, singing to the listener, not the theater; it became one man's experience, to be carried tenderly home and dreamed on. Billy Gaudens, whom Steyne had chosen to write the music for his revue, had tailor-made Lorette's numbers, fitting style and mood to the voice until they seemed of a piece. Gaudens had cleverly struck away from the prevailing beat and rock and folk sounds, going back to the impassioned ballads of Glory Guild's day — songs that grieved, demanded, yearned, sank to the roots. (Later, Ellery learned that all the other music in the show was in the modern idiom. Orrin Steyne was giving Lorette a showcase. He knew what he had.)

She's going to be a sensation, Ellery thought

. . . and, as he thought it, the old lightning struck.

More sensational than the girl.

He sat for a few moments, overwhelmed, thinking it over.

There was no doubt about it.

That's what GeeGee had meant.

He crept out of the orchestra seat and went groping for a phone.

THIRTY-FIVE

"Don't ask me why it hit me at Lorette's rehearsal," Ellery said an hour later in Wasser's office, to the attorney, his father, Harry Burke, and Roberta. "Or maybe it's because she makes music — I mean makes it! — and music is the secret of this thing."

"What thing?" demanded Inspector Queen. "What are you talking about, son?"

"Face," Ellery said. "The message GeeGee left on her desk as she was dying."

"What's music got to do with that?"

"Everything." Ellery was too hopped up to talk from a chair; he was darting about Wasser's office as if trying to dodge an assault of hornets. "I don't know how I could have been such a mental dropout. It was all there in those four letters.

"You'll note," he said, "that I say four *letters,* not the word. You'll note," he said, "that I use the word *note,* which is absolutely called for."

"You'll note, Mr. Queen," said Wasser, his tic ticking, "that you've already lost me."

"I'll find you again. Give me my head, Mr. Wasser. At times like these I feel as if I'd had ten drinks and then hit the fresh air. . . . Look.

212

"GeeGee wrote 'face.' It was evident that she meant 'face' as a reference to whoever shot her. It was also evident, and it's become increasingly so, as my headaches attest, that as a word-clue to her killer 'face' means nothing at all.

"The question naturally follows: Suppose it wasn't a word-clue?"

The Inspector frowned. "But if it wasn't a word-clue . . ."

"Exactly. If it wasn't a word-clue, what sort of clue could it be? This called for reexamination. I reexamined. I re-reexamined. I thought of everything it could be except what it is. And what it is is so obvious that none of us saw it at all.

"For if it wasn't a word-clue, it became simply a clue consisting of four letters of the English alphabet. Forming not a word, but a sequence of some sort, in some other frame of reference."

"A code?" the old man suggested.

"Don't interrupt me when I'm flying, please. Where was I? Oh, yes," Ellery said. "When you start thinking in those terms, it immediately strikes you that GeeGee wrote those four letters — wrote them physically — *as individual letters.* She separated them: *f* and a space, *a* and a space, *c* and a space, and finally *e.* True, spacing was characteristic of her handwriting generally; and to make it more misleading, the way she formed her letters made them look like hand printing rather than ordinary calligraphy. But once you think of *f-a-c-e* in some context other than words, you're in the clear and on your way."

"Not I," said Mrs. Burke's comfort-and-joy. The Scot frowned. "What context?"

"Well, what do we know about Glory Guild's preoccupations? One: as a performing artist, she spent her whole life in music. Two: in retirement she was a nut on puzzles. Right? Then think of f-a-c-e in terms of musicology and puzzles. A musical puzzle."

There was a silence, musical and puzzled. Ellery beamed; he had achieved orbital velocity, and as always at such times he was in a state of euphoria. His father, Wasser, Burke showed no signs of intelligence. Roberta West was cerebrating as if she were on to something — the big eyes were luminous under the indrawn sorrel brows — but finally she shook her bricktop.

"I studied music as a child, so I ought to know what you're getting at, Ellery. But I don't."

"What does f-a-c-e stand for in music, Roberta?"

"Face?"

"There's that old devil 'word' again. Not a word, Roberta. Letters. In music."

"Oh. You mean that f and a and c and e are notes?"

"What else? Of course that's what I mean. Which notes?"

"Which?"

"On the staff."

"If I had a sheet of music . . ."

"Mr. Wasser, may I?" Ellery grabbed a pad of plain yellow paper from the lawyer's desk, and a pen, and sketched quickly. When he held the pad up, they saw that he had inked in the common musical staff of five parallel lines:

"Here's the staff in G clef, the treble clef. Roberta, show us where the notes *f, a, c,* and *e* go."

Roberta took the pad and pen and, after some thought, used the pen.

"Now label each note."

She did so.

"Have a look." Ellery passed the pad around. What they saw was:

"So they're notes," said Inspector Queen. "And I take it Miss West's put them in the right places or you wouldn't be licking your chops. So what, Ellery?"

"The staff is composed of five lines and the four spaces between the lines. Where has Roberta placed the notes? On the lines or in the spaces?"

"In the spaces."

"In the *spaces*. Which means *between the lines*."

Ellery paused triumphantly.

"Are we supposed to put you up for mayor?" his father snapped. "I don't know what you're talking about, Ellery. You'll have to spell it out before it makes sense to my pea-brain."

"Wait." Harry Burke was gripping the arms of his chair. *"She was telling us to look between the lines."*

"Give the gentleman the cigar," Ellery said. "Yes, that was GeeGee's little musical-puzzle message. 'Look between the lines.' "

There was another silence.

"Which lines?" asked the Inspector wildly. "Where?"

"That, of course, is the question."

"Her diaries!"

"Logical, dad. But not reasonable. Remember how closely written her diaries are. Hardly any room on those jammed pages. She'd have to have had the talent of the man who wrote the Lord's Prayer on the head of a pin to have squeezed anything in between the lines of those entries."

"Then where? In one of her books?"

"Unlikely. There are hundreds of them."

"It couldn't be between the lines of anything handwritten," muttered Burke, "for the reason you gave. And yet not printing, either. Still it's got to be something mechanical, where the spacing is appreciable and regular . . ."

"You've got it, Harry."

Burke saw light.

"Something typewritten! Did she leave anything she'd typed?"

"Not necessarily that *she'd* typed."

"Her will," Wasser said slowly. "By God, her will!"

"That," Ellery nodded, "was my conclusion, too. That's why I asked for this meeting in your office, Mr. Wasser. When you read the will to the heirs you stated that the original was already in the hands of the Surrogate; you were reading from a copy. I recognized it as the one we found in the metal box in the Guild apartment, Glory's own copy. You still have it in your files?"

"Of course!"

"I'd like to have it."

While they waited for Wasser's secretary to fetch the will, Ellery remarked, "There's another reason for suspecting that Glory's copy of the will is the hiding place of some between-the-lines message from her . . . that long list of bequests to charities. It struck me at the time as peculiar. Why had she gone to the trouble of having all those trifling donations listed individually? A lump bequest could have been more conveniently provided for, to be parceled out at the discretion of her executor. But specifying the charities one by one did accomplish one thing — it made the will a much longer document, providing plenty of space for a considerable message. Ah, thank you," Ellery said to Wasser's secretary, taking the will. "Just a moment, please. Didn't I see an electric toaster in the outer office?"

"Yes, sir. Mr. Wasser often has his breakfast in the office. That's why we keep one here."

"I'd like to borrow it."

The girl brought it in, and Ellery plugged the connection into the wall behind the lawyer's desk. He set the toaster down on the desk and turned the machine on.

"Better than the match trick, eh?" Ellery said cheerfully. "Well, let's see if the old guesser is still functioning." He held the first page of the will above the heat coming up from the toast wells, passing the page back and forth. By this time they were crowding about him, craning.

"It's coming out!" Roberta cried.

In the spacing between the typewritten lines, the unmistakable handwriting of Glory Guild had begun to appear.

"I'll be damned," Harry Burke exclaimed.

"Somebody's going to be," Inspector Queen said exultantly. "Now maybe we'll get some-where on this case!"

THIRTY-SIX

It was a long message, as Ellery had predicted, written for economy in minute calligraphy. It occupied the spaces between the lines on all but the bottom half of the last typewritten page.

"Dad, you read it."

Ellery sat quietly down.

    I am writing this

the Inspector read aloud

for reasons that will become clear soon enough. I had wanted for some time to get away from things, and I had planned to go up to Newtown, to the cottage. I asked Carlos to drive up with me, but he begged off, saying, he was not feeling well. I fussed with his headache until he said he felt a bit better, so it was not until late afternoon that I left. (I wanted to call the trip off, but Carlos insisted that I go.)

When I got to the cottage I found that the electricity was not turned on, even though I had insructed Jeanne several days before to notify Connecticut Light & Power to restore service (I later found out that she'd simply forgotten, which was not like Jeanne at all). I would have made do with candles, except that the house was very damp and cold — the heating is electric, too. Rather than risk a virus (do singers ever get over their fear of colds?) I decided to turn right around and go back to the city.

I took the penthouse elevator up and I was about to put my key in the lock when I heard voices from the living room, Carlos's and a woman's. The woman's voice was that of a stranger. It was a shock. In my own home! He had no shame, no shame. I was furious, sick, and disgusted.

I went downstairs again and took the service elevator up, and I let myself in through the kitchen and pantry and listened from behind the dining room door. Carlos and the woman were still talking away. The door is a swinging door, and I pushed it open a crack and peeped in. I am not proud of myself about all this, but I could have strangled Carlos for having lied about not feeling well, and entertaining a woman in my home the moment I was out of the way, and I wanted to see what she looked like. She was young, and small, and fair, with red hair and tiny hands and feet (and I'm such a horse! — or rather "cow," as I heard my dear husband refer to me to this girl, a cow "to be milked," he told her).

Roberta West went blue-white. "That was me," she breathed. "That must have been the night he . . . And she was listening at the door! What must she have thought of me!" Harry Burke took her hand and shushed her.

Inspector Queen read on, glaring at Roberta:

Carlos was doing most of the talking and the long and short of it is that *he was plotting against my life.* I am not imagining this; he spelled it out. My knees began to shake, and I remember thinking, "No, this is a joke, he can't be serious." I almost walked in on them to tell him what a bad joke I thought it was. But I didn't. Something held me back. I continued to eavesdrop, hating myself and yet unable to tear myself away.

He told this girl that if he did it himself he would be the first to be suspected. So he had to have a real alibi. (By this time I wasn't so sure he was joking.) He then proposed to the girl that *she* do the actual killing while he established his alibi, and that after he inherited all my money he would marry her and they'd live happily ever after. So it was no joke after all. He meant it. He really meant it.

I couldn't take any more. I ran out through the kitchen, leaving them in the living room, and down the service elevator, and I walked and walked, not knowing what to do, where to go, whom to turn to. I walked most of the night. Then I took my car and drove back to Newtown and had the power turned on and stayed at the cottage for two whole days, thinking things out. And not getting any-where, I might add. If I went to the police, what good would it do? It would be my word against his, with the girl's denial to back him up; it would get into the papers and create a horrid mess. Anyway, the most I could expect from the police would be somebody to guard me, but they couldn't do that indefi-nitely, even if they believed me.

I could divorce him. But by this time I was over the shock and most of the fears. I was fighting mad. I knew what Carlos was, of course, and I suspected that he was chasing other women, but murder! I never dreamed he would bloody his hands. There was an unreality about the whole thing, anyway. All I could think of was that I had to get back at him some way, that would badly hurt him. Divorce wouldn't do it the way I wanted it done. He had to think everything was going his way.

Of course, I was gambling with my life. Maybe in my heart of hearts I didn't really believe it. Anyway, I've lived the best part of my life, and if it's cut short by a few years . . . It will make no sense to anyone but another woman, who's grown old and ugly and fat and forgotten after having had everything, admiration and applause and fame and everything wonderful that goes with them.

I kept my eyes very wide open after that and soon found out that my suspicions about Carlos and other women were all too well-founded. He's even seduced Jeanne Temple, my secretary, poor thing; no wonder she's been so nervous. I don't blame the women, Carlos has something that women can't resist. Of course, I had *not* torn up our prenuptial agreement, because of my suspicions. I'd fooled him into thinking I had. Keeping it in force gives me another weapon against him, the hurtiest one of all.

I have other weapons, too — this new will, on which I'm writing in disappearing ink. I've also left a clue in invisible ink on my diary page for December first. This is all in case I am murdered. I don't know what Carlos is waiting for, maybe just the right opportunity — I haven't given him many! But something tells me the time is drawing near, something about the way he's been acting. If I'm right about his intentions, and I am convinced I am, he'll get what he deserves, and where it will hurt the most. One of the things I have done is start a search for my sister's only child, Lorette Spanier. I've left the bulk of my estate to her. That ought to wipe the charm off Carlos's face! I'd love to be able to be there when this will is read to him.

To whoever reads this: If I should die a violent death, my husband is the one who arranged it. Even though he will have some alibi, he's as guilty as if he did it with his own hands. The woman will be just his tool.

I have been trying to find out who the girl is who was in my apartment the night I overheard him plan my murder, but Carlos has been very coy about her. As far as I can tell he hasn't seen her again, unless it's been on the sly. So I do not know her name, although I have the oddest feeling I have seen her somewhere before. Here is her description: Late twenties, very fair skin, red hair, height about five feet three, cute figure, pretty eyes (I couldn't tell the color), speaks with a stagy diction (could I have seen her somewhere around Broadway, or on tour?), and she dresses sort of Greenwich Villagey. She has a prominent birthmark on her right cheek, high up, shaped like an almost perfect butterfly, that ought to make her easy to identify. This girl is Carlos's accomplice. She is the one who, if I am murdered, will have done the murder for him.

Signed — Glory Guild

Inspector Queen looked up from the last page. He squinted at Roberta's birthmark and shrugged. Then the old man set the will down on Wasser's desk and turned away.

"Butterfly birthmark," Harry Burke exclaimed.

"That's why she thought Roberta looked familiar. Didn't you say, Bertie, you'd met her with Armando that time in summer stock? It must have stuck in her mind."

"But she got it all wrong," Roberta said in a quavery voice. "She must have run out of the apartment that night in May before she heard me turn Carlos down cold and leave. If she'd stayed another few minutes, she'd have known that I told him I wanted no part of it or him. She'd never have written this. Not about me, anyway."

Burke cradled her hand. "Of course not, Bertie."

"And she wasn't able to track me down because I never saw Carlos again until the night of the murder, when he turned up at my apartment to use me as his alibi!" The pink butterfly on her cheek was fluttering in distress. "God, how did I ever get into this?"

Burke was glaring at Ellery as if he expected words of wisdom or at least of comfort. But Ellery was low in his chair, nuzzling his knuckles, sucking on them and getting no sustenance.

Nobody said anything for a long time.

"So," Inspector Queen ultimately muttered, "we're all the way back to where we were. Further back. The one clue we had is a dud. Gets us not an inch closer to the woman Armando had pull the job."

"But this is evidence against him, Inspector," Wasser protested. "Now you have not only Miss

225

West's testimony, but Glory Guild's documented corroboration of Armando's proposal to Miss West as well."

But the Inspector shook his head. "To put Armando away, Mr. Wasser, we need the woman. I notice," he added with a sour glance at his son, "that you're not saying anything."

"What's there to say?" Ellery mumbled. "You've said it all, dad. We'll have to start from scratch again."

THIRTY-SEVEN

Start again they did, and scratch they did, and what they garnered for their pains was a wealth of hindsight that told them nothing they had not known before. In addition to which Armando was being shrewdly difficult.

He was no longer seeing Mrs. Ardene (Piggy-back) Vlietland, the lady of the Newport $100,000 brawl. Mrs. Gertie Hodge Huppenkleimer of Chicago and Beekman Place was no longer seeing him; apparently her taste for used toys had turned toward newer and safer amusements and Armando was making no attempts visible to the probing eye to resume their play. Horsewoman and alcoholic Daffy Dingle was still drying out up around Boston way. Armando had also dropped Jeanne Temple, who was reported mooning about the East 49th Street apartment she shared with Virginia Whiting and going out on an occasional part-time secretarial job, her brief amour no doubt nursed to her impressive chest. Dr. Susan Merckell seemed too busy with ailing larynges at large to fiddle with Armando's or his throat was suddenly in perfect health. Marta Bellina was off again, in Europe somewhere, on another singing tour. They did not even bother with Selma Pilter; Armando had younger fish to fry. And there was nothing, utterly nothing, on the mysterious woman in the violet veil, or any veil at all. It was as if she had been something out of a gothic romance, drifting about in limbo, the creation of someone's overheated imagination.

Armando was concentrating on Lorette Spanier, playing the role of avuncular confessor and nurseryman of a tender talent. He attended her rehearsals regularly, sitting in the empty orchestra of the Roman Theater while she tried out a new Billy Gaudens number or worked on a classic; appearing like magic backstage when she was through for the day; taking her home or to some hideaway restaurant if she was not too exhausted; soothing her when she was in a mopy mood over the way things were going. He was seen with her everywhere.

"The little fool," Harry Burke snorted. "Doesn't she have the most elementary sense of caution?"

"She's lonely, Harry," Roberta said. "You just don't understand women."

"I understand the Armandos of this world!"

"So," said Roberta grimly, "do I. But don't judge Lorette by your great big masculine standards, my love. She'll find a way to take care of herself. Most of us do; it's an instinct women are born with. Right now she needs somebody to lean on and talk to. Carlos makes that kind of thing awfully easy."

Burke snorted.

"He'll take her the way he took her aunt."

"He didn't really take Glory Guild, did he? Not according to that secret message of hers."

"Then why is she lying in a copper-lined box, not breathing?"

"He isn't going to harm Lorette. He wants her money."

"And he'll get it, too!"

"Not for a long time, darling. Don't sell little Lorette short. She may be making a fool of herself with Carlos right now, but she'll let it go only just so far. To get the money he's got to marry her, and I have the feeling he's not going to find Lorette that gullible."

"He talked her aunt into it!"

"Her aunt was practically an old woman. Lorette's not only loaded, she's young and beautiful. This is just a phase. Anyway, why spend all this time talking about *them?* I've got to get up early tomorrow morning."

So they turned to other things, which left them both breathing hard.

Roberta had been accepted for an off-Broadway play, in which she had not a line to say; she was to appear for three interminable acts, upstage right, in a flesh-colored bikini, doing the frug. "The author tells me he wrote it while under the influence of LSD," she told Burke. "And you know what? I believe him." She crept home each night battered in every muscle and sinew.

They were consequently hard times for the

Scot. While Roberta rehearsed, he spent most of his days with Ellery, hanging uselessly about police headquarters. They came to resemble a pair out of low tragedy, detesting the sight of each other, but bound together by an unseverable bond, like Siamese twins.

Their dialogue was dreary.

"Are you as sick of me as I am of you?" Ellery demanded.

"Righto," Burke snapped.

"Then why don't you cut out?"

"I can't, Ellery. Why don't you?"

"I can't, either."

"My pal."

"Put it there, pal."

Burke put his hands into his pockets.

Inspector Queen went pathetically to see the district attorney.

"How about hauling Armando before the grand jury without the woman, Herman?"

The D.A. shook his head.

"But we've got Glory's story between those lines," the Inspector argued. "We've got Roberta West's testimony." He was really arguing with himself, using the D.A. as a sounding board.

"So what, Dick? All they prove is possible intention on his part seven months before the fact. Even if I could get a grand jury to indict, which I doubt, can't you imagine what a good defense lawyer would do to my case? And you know Armando would hire the best. If you ask me, Dick, the bastard would enjoy the publicity. I'm

230

damned if I'm going to give it to him without a fighting chance to put him away. The only chance we've got is that woman."

"What woman?" the Inspector whined. "I'm beginning to think she never existed."

Pathetic or not, the Inspector refused to give up. He summoned Carlos Armando to head-quarters with cunning regularity — to keep his teeth on edge, the old warrior told Ellery and Harry Burke. But if the summonses to Centre Street were designed to fray Armando's nerves, they frayed only the Inspector's. The man seemed to thrive on the visits. He no longer howled harassment or threatened legal action. He was charming, his negative answers were oiled with courtesy, his blunt teeth grinned, and once he even offered the old man a cigar. ("I don't smoke cigars," the Inspector rasped, "and if I did I wouldn't smoke one from Havana, and if I did I wouldn't accept it from you, Armando, and if I did I'd choke on it." Armando thereupon offered the cigar to Ellery, who thoughtfully took it. "I'll pass it along to some rat I want to poison," he said to Armando with equal courtesy. Armando smiled.)

"He's got me by the short hairs," yelled the In-spector, "and he's loving every minute of it. Keeps asking me why I don't arrest him! I've never hated anyone so much in my life. I wish I'd gone in for a career in the Sanitation Depart-ment." At their puzzled looks he added, "At least I'd be equipped to handle this garbage."

The old man stopped calling Armando down to Centre Street.

Burke asked: "Then it's going into the unsolved file?"

"Not on your tintype," the Inspector snapped; he always fell back on the slang of his youth when he was upset. "I'll stick with this case till they shovel me under. But these sessions are giving me ulcers, not him. We'll lie low for a while and hope he gets too pleased with himself. Maybe he'll make a mistake. Maybe one of these days he'll contact the woman. Or she'll contact him. I've got him under twenty-four-hour surveillance."

And not only by Inspector Queen's squad. Ellery, who was losing weight he could not afford, took to trailing along with the trailers, or independently, lightening the burden on his bathroom scale still further. He saw a great deal of the Playboy Club and the Gaslight Club and Danny's Hideaway and Dinty Moore's and Sardi's and Lindy's, and even more of the musty interior of the Roman Theater, and had nothing to show for it but acid stomach and an occasional hangover.

"Then why do you do it?" Harry Burke asked him.

"You know what they say about hope," Ellery shrugged. "It's a cinch I can't do any work."

"The old game," Burke sighed. "See who has more patience, the fox or the hounds. Nothing?"

"Nothing. Want to join me in this exercise in futility?"

"No, thank you. I haven't the stomach for it, Ellery. Sooner or later I'd throttle him. Anyway, there's Roberta."

There was Roberta, and Burke suddenly had better things to do than fume in Ellery's presence, being fumed back at. One night, when Roberta crawled into her hole in-the-wall from the Village hole-in-the-wall where she had frugged onstage all day, and consequently was in no condition to resist a decent human emotion, the Scot took his courage in both brawny hands, like one of his forebears' claymores, and swung wildly.

"Bertie. Bert. Roberta. I can't stand this any longer. I mean, you can say what you like about police dogs, but they lead a damned dullish life. I'm going out of my mind, Roberta. Hanging about. I mean . . ."

"You mean you want to go *home*," Roberta said with a little cry.

"Definitely! You understand, don't you?"

"Oh, yes," Roberta said, with the thinnest layer of ice on her voice. It was her best stage voice, the one she had always yearned to employ in an interpretation of Lady Macbeth. "I certainly do."

Burke beamed. "Then it's all settled." Then he said anxiously, "Isn't it?"

"What's settled?"

"I thought —"

To his horror, Roberta began to blub. "Oh, I

233

don't blame you, Harry . . ."

"Bertie! What on earth's the matter?"

"N-nothing."

"There *is*. Or you wouldn't be crying, for the love of God."

"I'm *not* crying! Why should I cry, for the love of God? Of course you want to go home. You're in a land of aliens. No dart games in the pubs, no Rockers or Mods, no changing of the Guard . . . Harry, please. I have a headache. Good night."

"But." Burke's transparent eyes let some honest bewilderment through. "But I thought . . ." He stopped.

"Yes. You're always thinking. You're so cerebral, Harry." Roberta suddenly turned over on the couch cover she was blubbing into. "You thought what?"

"I thought you'd realize that I didn't mean —"

"You *didn't* mean? You're so exasperating sometimes, Harry. Can't you talk simple, understandable English?"

"I'm Scots," Burke said stiffishly. "We don't speak the same language, perhaps but what I have in mind is supposed to be universal. What I didn't mean — I mean, what I meant was . . ."

"Yes, Harry?"

"Damn it all to hell!" Burke's wrestler's neck was purple with strain. "I want you to go home with me!"

Roberta was sitting up by this time, frowning a little at the mess she found her hair in. "That would be nice, Harry. I mean under different circumstances. I mean you're not very clever about propositioning girls, you don't have the *savoir-faire* of men like Carlos, or even Ellery Queen, but I suppose I ought to take it as a compliment, considering the source. You are a darling in your own way. Are you actually proposing to unclasp your purse to finance a trip to England for me in return for my illegal embraces? I couldn't afford it on my own, of course, though I'd love to see England; I've always dreamed of going there — Stratford-on-Avon and all that. But, darling, I'm afraid I can't take you up on it. I see I've given you the wrong impression of myself. Just because circumstances forced me to confess that I'd once had an affair with that monster Carlos doesn't give you the right to think I'm that kind of girl generally. But you are sweet, Harry; thank you at least for wanting a few nights of love with me. And now, really, I am tired and I'd like to go to bed — alone. Good night, Harry."

"*Will — you — be — quiet!*" the Scot roared. "You don't understand at all! I want to marry you!"

"Oh, Harry," Roberta cried. "If I'd only known!"

Whatever other mendacity she was about to utter was never uttered. The rest was smothered in powerful arms and lips.

"Well, old chap," Burke told Ellery the next day with bashful jubilance, "I finally popped the old question."

235

Ellery grunted. "How did Roberta get it out of you?"

"Beg your pardon?"

"The poor girl's been waiting for you to pop it for weeks. Maybe months for all I know. Anyone but a lovesick Scot would have seen it. Congratulations." Ellery shook Burke's hand limply.

They were planning to be married as soon as the avant garde turkey Roberta was rehearsing for opened and closed, which Miss West predicted would be in nothing flat. "And we're going to bow our necks to the yoke in Merrie Olde," Burke cried. "Can't wait for that BOAC flight, chappie. To tell you the truth, I've had a bellyful of your lovely country."

"Sometimes," Ellery nodded wistfully, "I wish you'd licked us at Yorktown."

And he cursed Carlos Armando and all his gypsy ancestors, and went back to his novel.

THIRTY-EIGHT

Orrin Steyne's revue opened to notices that read as though they had been scribbled during an orgasm rather than sedately composed in its aftermath. It had been an uninspired theatrical season, and the time was hot for critical passion.

Or perhaps it was the legendary Orrin Steyne luck. He had never had a flop; and, in the unkind little world in which theatrical producers lived and labored, success was spitefully expressed in gambling terms, not in the context of a talent for the game.

About Lorette Spanier there could be no semantics. A performer by definition performed; the only question was how well. The answer, headlined and shouted, was unequivocal. The critics acclaimed her Broadway's latest love, *Variety* said STEYNE FIND BOFFO, Walter Kerr himself pronounced her the logical successor to Glory Guild, *Life* scheduled a profile of her, the in-groups debated whether she was high camp or low, and the squares queued up at the box office and laid siege to the stage door to fight for her autograph. Selma Pilter got her Lorette Spanier on a management contract — the old woman had been working on an oral understanding —

with Armando's instant blessing: "You are better off signed with Selma, *cara,* than letting yourself be exposed to every sharpie in this cutthroat business." And there was a cherished cable from West Berlin: I TOLD YOU TO KEEP PROJECTING LOVE MARTA.

The revue opened on a Thursday night. Friday afternoon Ellery telephoned Kip Kipley's unlisted number.

"Can you get me two tickets for Orrin Steyne's *Revue*? I've tried everywhere with no luck."

"When do you want them for, a year from Christmas?" the columnist asked.

"Saturday night."

"*This* Saturday night?"

"This Saturday night."

"Who do you think I am, Jackie Kennedy?" said Kipley. Then he said, "I'll see what I can do." He called back in ten minutes. "Why I scratch your back when you still owe me God knows how much *pro quo* I'll never understand. They'll be at the box office."

"Thanks, Kip."

"You can shove your thanks, Charlie. Give me something I can print, and we're buddy-buddies."

"I wish I could," Ellery sighed, and hung up. He really did.

For, novel and deadline notwithstanding, the Guild case kept niggling him. He had no idea why he had suddenly decided to see the revue. The decision had nothing to do with the magnitude of Lorette's talent; he was willing to take Broadway's word for that. And as a rule he avoided musicals. Still, putting it down to a vague professional itch to keep his finger on the pulse of the cadaver, Ellery took his father by the resisting arm — to the girly-girly-brought-up Inspector, musicals had died with Florenz Ziegfeld and Earl Carroll; he had thought *Oklahoma!* rather dull and *My Fair Lady* a lot of fancy nonsense — and on Saturday evening they set off for the Roman Theater.

Their taxi had to fight the usual good fight with the traffic (no New Yorker in his right mind took a private car into the theater district on Saturday nights); they exchanged the usual nostalgia-spiked imprecations on the honkytonk atmosphere of the new Times Square; they did the usual elbow work on the neighborly line at the THIS PERFORMANCE window of the old Roman; and eventually they found themselves seated in the orchestra on the aisle, sixth row center, that Valhalla of the hit-show devotee's dreams.

"Mighty nice," the Inspector said, partially mollified. "How did you do it?" He did not know about Ellery's appeal to Kipley. "These seats must have set you back half a week's salary. My salary, anyway."

Ellery said sententiously, "Money isn't everything," and settled back with the playbill. There were some things a man didn't tell, even to his father.

And there it was. *Songs.* . . . *Lorette Spanier*, at the end of the first act. Everyone in their vicinity, it seemed, had the program open to the same page; Ellery squinted here and there to make sure. It happened once every ten years or so, that lightning something in the air of old theaters that smelled like brimstone. It could be detected only at the birth of a new star. You could almost hear the crackle of the sparks.

Even that died away after the blackout preceding her appearance, leaving a silence so heavy it seemed about to burst from its own weight.

The darkness was as palpable as the silence.

Ellery found himself crouched on the edge of his seat. He felt his father, the least impressionable of men, doing the same thing beside him.

No one shuffled or coughed.

A tall pure white cone suddenly sprang down from the proscenium to center stage. Bathed in its brilliant light sat Lorette, at a vast rose piano, pale hands folded. A black velvet backdrop with a gigantic American Beauty rose embroidered on it was her background. She was dressed in a flashing sequined evening gown of the same color as the rose, with a high neckline and no back at all. She wore no jewelry, and her white skin and golden hair seemed stamped on the velvet. She was looking, not at the audience, but at the hands in her lap. It was as if she were all alone somewhere, listening for something not audible to ordinary ears.

She held her indrawn pose for fully thirty seconds. Then she looked up and at the conductor in the well. He raised his baton, holding it aloft deliberately. When it came down, the orchestra burst into an anguished fortissimo chord, heavily brassed and there were gasps.

All at once the chord segued into the soft teasing introduction to Gauden's already acclaimed "Where O Where?" The introduction died away, and Lorette raised her hands. She played a swift caressing arpeggio, threw her shining head back, and began to sing.

It was very nearly the same voice Ellery had listened to on that day of rehearsal, but not quite. A dimension had been added, an intangible something that made the difference between quality and style. Whether she had soared to the challenge of her opportunity, or Marta Bellina had taught her some unique secret of the singer's art, the fact was that Lorette now had both. The quality was Glory Guild's; the style was Lorette's own. In that sense Walter Kerr had been precisely right. In the same way that a generation sprang from its parents, carrying their genes but adding combinatons of its own to become something altogether new, the niece was indeed "the logical successor" to her aunt.

There was the old Guild vocal intimacy, inner-directed to the individual ear in its faintly throbbing passion; what made it new was a curious preoccupation with self that Guild had never had, as if Lorette were conscious of no audience at all, the inner direction being result rather than cause. It was as if she were singing to herself in the privacy of her bedroom, allowing herself an erotic freedom of expression that she would not have dreamed of expressing in public. It turned every man and woman in the audience into a sort of Listening Tom, ear squeezed to a forbidden door; it raised the blood pressure and made breathing difficult.

It was smashing.

Fighting the effect on his nervous system, Ellery tore his attention away from what was happening to him to observe what was happening to the people around him. His father was pressed forward, eyes half shut, with a grin on his old lips that had pain as well as remembered pleasure in it. The few others he could make out in the near darkness were just as embarrassing to behold. Each face was stripped of social controls, oblivious of decencies and restraints, nakedly isolated. It was not a pretty sight, and it revolted as well as fascinated him. My God, Ellery thought, she'll become a destructive social force, she'll turn neighborly communities into packs of slavering lone wolves, she'll disperse the herd yearnings of the young and replace marijuana and LSD in the college dorms. She could not possibly realize the dangerous potentialities of her power. She'll sell tens of millions of records and there ought to be a law against her.

There were five other songs: "Love, Love"; "You're Trouble to Me"; "There's No Moon

Ever"; "Take Me"; and "I Want to Die" . . .

Lorette's hands returned to her lap.

The roar that shook the theater she did not acknowledge; she did not even look around. She simply sat there, as she had begun, hands folded, eyes lowered, lost in her own echoes. This was at Orrin Steyne's direction, Ellery was sure, but he did not think she would have reacted differently had Steyne never said a word.

They would not allow her to stop. The first-act curtain came down, went up, came down, went up again; still she sat there, a glittering little figure at the great piano on the otherwise empty stage.

More! *More! MORE!*

It became a thunderous growl.

Lorette swung about on the bench then, all flashing rose in the spotlight; for the first time she looked her audience in the eye.

The ploy was startling. It brought instant silence.

"I should so much like to sing and sing for you," she murmured. "But there's a great deal more of Mr. Steyne's wonderful show in store, so I have time for only one encore. I don't believe Billy Gaudens will mind if I reach far back into the past. This song lyric was written by someone you probably remember in a field worlds away from music, James J. Walker; the music was by Ernest R. Ball. It was first published in 1905, and it was revived and became famous in the late Twenties, when Jimmy Walker was Mayor of New York. It was a very special favorite of Glory Guild's — my aunt."

A shrewd stroke of Steyne's — Ellery was positive Steyne had inspired it — this uttering GeeGee Guild's name aloud, hauling into the light what lurked in the darkness of everyone's thoughts.

Lorette turned back to her piano.

The same electric silence crackled.

The same breaths were withheld.

She began to sing once more.

It was perhaps an unfortunate choice musically and lyrically. Ball's music was sticky sweet; Walker's lyric, especially of the verse, evoked images of birds in gilded cages and poor sewing-machine girls:

> Now in the summer of life, sweetheart,
> You say you love but me,
> Gladly I give all my heart to you,
> Throbbing with ecstasy.
> But last night I saw while a-dreaming,
> The future old and gray,
> And I wondered if you'll love me then,
>   dear,
> Just as you do today.

Refrain (*molto espressivo*):

> Will you love me in December as you do
>   in May,
> Will you love me in the good
>   old-fashioned way?

When my hair has all turned gray,
Will you kiss me then, and say,
That you love me in December as you
do in May?

Lorette gave it *molto espressivo,* English music hall style. Ellery shook his head. It was a mistake, and he was willing to bet that before many performances had passed Orrin Steyne — or Billy Gaudens — would see to it that Lorette's encore number was less in the nature of a parody. From the throat of any other singer he could think of the song would have aroused smiles, if not titters. It was a tribute to Lorette's power that her audience was as passionately rapt by this song from another world and time as they had been by Gauden's cunning music.

Listening to Beau James's youthful effusion — *Beau James* was what Gene Fowler had entitled his biography of Jimmy Walker — Ellery was reminded that the theme of Walker's sentimental lyric, especially that of the chorus, had evidently haunted him to his dying day. According to Fowler, some four decades after the original publication of "Will You Love Me in December As You Do in May?" which Lorette Spanier was now singing almost twenty years still later, as the one-time Tin Pan Alley aspirant, trial lawyer, state senator, mayor, and playboy politico sat in his darkened room during his last illness, he had suddenly turned on a light, reached for a pencil, and begun to compose the lyric to a new song. It

245

had concluded with the lines:

> There'll be no December
> If you'll just remember,
> Sweetheart, it's always May.

After four decades and two world wars Jimmy Walker had come full circle.

I wish, Ellery found himself thinking, I could do the same with the Guild case.

There'll be no December . . .

Ellery sat up as though touched by a live wire. As indeed, in a way, he had been. The coincidence would have been amusing in other circumstances. He had shifted his left elbow on the arm of his seat, and the movement had caused the sharp edge of the seat's arm to press into the hollow behind his elbow and the sensitive nerve beneath. The unpleasant shock almost made him cry out.

Inspector Queen shushed him angrily, intent on the song. To the Inspector, what Lorette was singing was a piece of his youth.

But to Ellery it was a foretaste of the immediate future. He would almost have cried out even if the nerve had not been shocked. For he was shocked in a far more vulnerable place.

"Dad."

"Shut up!" his father hissed.

"Dad, we'll have to leave."

"What?"

"At least I'll have to."

246

"Are you out of your mind? Now, damn it, you've made me lose the end of the song!" Lorette had finished, and the applause rose from all around them in crashing waves. She rose from the bench and stood unsmiling, white hand on the end of the rose piano, blue eyes glittering in the spot; all of her glittered. Then the curtain came down, and it stayed down. The house lights went up.

"I swear I can't imagine what comes over you," the old man complained as they shoved their way up the aisle. "You're a natural-born spoiler, Ellery. Man, what a voice!" He went on and on about Lorette; or perhaps it was about himself.

Ellery said nothing until they reached the crowded lobby. He was scowling in some sort of pain. "You don't have to go, dad. Why not stay and see the rest of the show? I'll meet you back home later."

"Wait a minute, will you? What's eating you?"

"I just remembered something."

"About the Guild case?" the old man asked instantly.

"Yes."

"What?"

"I'd rather not say yet. I have to check something first. You really don't have to leave, dad. I don't want to spoil your night out."

"You've already spoiled it. Anyway, I don't care about the rest of the show. I've had my money's worth, and then some. What a singer!

247

About the Guild case?"

"The Guild case."

"It bugs me, too," the old man said. "Where we going?"

"Didn't you turn over that copy of Glory Guild's will to the D.A.? The one with the secret writing on it that we brought out in Wasser's office?"

"Yes?"

"I'll have to find him."

"Wasser?"

"The D.A."

"Herman? Now? On Saturday night?"

Ellery nodded morosely.

Inspector Queen glanced at him sidewise and said nothing more. They shouldered their way out into 47th Street, ducked into a nearby restaurant, located its public phone, and Ellery spent twenty-five minutes tracking down the district attorney. It turned out that he was attending a political banquet at the Waldorf, and he sounded nasty over the phone. The banquet was getting full press and TV coverage.

"Now?" he said to Ellery. "On Saturday night?"

"Yes, Herman," Ellery said.

"Can't it wait till Monday morning, for God's sake?"

"No, Herman," Ellery said.

"Stop sounding like the straight man in a vaudeville routine," the D.A. snapped. "All right, Mystery Man, I'll meet you and the In-

248

spector down in my office as soon as I can get there. But this better be good!"

"Good is not the word for it," Ellery muttered, and hung up.

THIRTY-NINE

By the time he got through reading the minute chirography between the typewritten lines of Glory Guild's copy of her will, Ellery looked ten years older. "Well?" the district attorney demanded. "Did you find what you were looking for?"

"I found it."

"Found what, son?" the Inspector wanted to know. "When I read it aloud in Wasser's office that day, I didn't leave out or change a word. What's the point?"

"That's the point. You two give me some slack on this, will you?"

"You mean to say you're not going to talk even now?" his father growled.

"Gets me away from that banquet with all the news media there," the D.A. said to his ceiling, "on a Saturday night yet, with my wife wondering if I've gone off with a chick somewhere, and he won't open up! Thank God, Dick, I'm not stuck with a kook for a son. I'm going back to the Waldorf, and I won't be available for *anything* till Monday morning — not if I want to hold onto my wife, and I want to. When this joker is ready to let a mere servant of the people in on whatever he's trick-or-treating, let me know. Be sure you lock my door on your way out."

"Well?" Inspector Queen asked in the silence of the shadowy office after its rightful owner left.

"Not now, dad," Ellery mumbled, "not yet."

The old man shrugged. It was an old story to him, and he had learned to live with it.

They went home in a silent taxicab.

Eventually the Inspector left his pride and joy in an equally silent study, pulling on his celebrated lower lip and staring down some mysterious tunnel inhabited, to judge from his expression, by particularly revolting monsters.

FORTY

So the mystery's face rotated past its three-quarter position, and Ellery saw the whole face at last, and knew it.

4 FULL FACE

"Bury me on my face," said Diogenes; and when he was asked why, he replied, "Because in a little while everything will be turned upside down."

DIOGENES LAERTIUS

FORTY-ONE

The Inspector shook him awake.

"What?" Ellery shouted, shooting up in bed.

"I haven't said anything yet," his father said. "Get up, will you? You have company."

"What time is it?"

"Eleven o'clock, and the day is Sunday, in case you forgot. What time did you get to bed?"

"I don't know, dad. Four, five, something like that. Company? Who?"

"Harry Burke and Roberta West. If you ask me," the Inspector grumbled from the doorway, "those two are plotting something. They look too damn happy to be up to anything legal."

They did indeed. The Scot was sucking on a dead pipe furiously, his sandy brows working like pistons, his wrestler's neck mottled in a flaming purple motif, and his transparent eyes doing a sort of optical hornpipe. In his blunt right hand nestled Roberta's left, being ground up and loving every bone-crushing moment of it. Ellery had never seen Roberta so vivacious. She bubbled over the instant he came shambling out in his faded old dressing gown and down-at-heel slippers.

"Guess what, Ellery?" Roberta cried. "We're getting married!"

"Am I supposed to go into a Highland fling?" Ellery grunted. "That earth-shaking event was announced to me some time ago."

"But we've changed our *plans*, Ellery."

"We're not going to wait until Bertie's show closes to go to England," said Burke excitedly. "She's chucked the bloody thing, and we're going to be married here and now."

"In my apartment?" Ellery asked sourly.

"I don't mean here and now," Burke said, "meaning New York and today."

"Oh?" Ellery perked up. "And what caused this change in strategy? Sit down, please, both of you. I can't abide people who jump about first thing Sunday morning. Dad, is there any tomato juice in the fridge? I need lots of tomato juice this morning."

"It's Harry," Roberta said, slipping into one of the chairs at the dinette table in the alcove of the living room. "He's so masterful. He couldn't wait."

"Bloody well could not," Burke said, seating himself by her side and recapturing her hand. "Said to myself, 'Why wait?' Makes no bloody sense, when you think of it. And I've thought of bloody little else. All we need is a dominie and it's done."

"You also need a little thing called a marriage license," Ellery said, "— thanks, dad!" He took a long gulp of the bloody stuff. "Wasserman, three

256

days, and all that. How do you propose to do it all today?"

"Oh, we've got the tests over with and the license now for a week," Roberta said. "Do you suppose I might have a smidge of that, Inspector? It looks so good, and I haven't had any breakfast. Or dinner last night, come to think of it. Harry was so insistent."

"Don't put it all on Harry," Ellery said disagreeably; "he couldn't take the Wasserman for you. Well, I guess it's congratulations again. Is there anything I can do?"

"You don't sound very enthusiastic," Harry Burke growled. "Don't you approve?"

"Slip the chip, chum," Ellery said. "Why should I be enthusiastic over your marriage? Eggs, dad. Do we have any eggs?"

"Thank you, Inspector!" said Roberta. She sipped thirstily.

"Coming up," the Inspector said. "Anybody else?"

"I'd *love* some," Roberta said breathlessly, lowering the tomato juice. "Wouldn't you, Harry?"

"Come on, Bertie." Burke glared at Ellery. "I'll take you out to breakfast."

"Harry."

"Simmer down, Harry," Ellery said. "I'm not at my best Sunday mornings. Dad makes the meanest scrambled eggs on the West Side. Have some. Come on."

"No, thank you," Burke said stiffly.

"And *lots* of toast, Inspector, please," Roberta

257

said. "Harry, stop being a drag."

"Coming up," the Inspector said again, and disappeared in the kitchen again.

"He could show some enthusiasm," Burke complained. "What's the matter with Sunday mornings?"

"The matter is that they come after Saturday nights," Ellery explained. "This particular Saturday night I didn't get to bed until well into Sunday morning."

"Conscience, a head, or a lively bit of fluff? Or all three?"

"Dad and I saw Orrin Steyne's *Revue* last night."

Burke looked puzzled. "What of it? So did a great many other people, and from what I hear they enjoyed themselves. Sometimes you make no sense, Ellery."

"There was a song Lorette sang . . ." Ellery stopped. "Never mind. We were talking about your shotgun nuptials." He suddenly seemed to have swallowed something bitter.

Roberta looked indignant.

"Shotgun! I don't know where private detectives get their reputations. A girl is safer with Harry than with a dedicated violet. Harry and I debated whether to go see her or not," Roberta went on, failing to signal a righthand turn, "and don't the eggs and bacon smell yummy. And is there anything more delicious than toast making? Is she as good as they're saying, Ellery?"

"What? Oh. Sensational."

"Then we won't go. I can't stand other people's success. That's something you'll find out about me, Harry. We couldn't go, anyway. We'll be in England —"

"Now that spring is here," Burke and Ellery said in unison. Whereupon Burke grinned, stuck his hand across the table, and called out, "Put some more eggs on, Inspector! I've changed my mind."

"Nuptials," Ellery reminded them glumly. "Who's committing the crime?"

"That," Roberta said, frowning, "happens to be our problem. Realize what day it is today?"

"Certainly, it's Sunday." At her reproving look Ellery said, "Isn't it?"

"What Sunday?"

"*What* Sunday?"

"It's Palm Sunday, that's what Sunday."

"So it is." Ellery looked chagrined. "I'm not following, I think. Palm Sunday?"

"Heathen! Palm Sunday is the beginning of Holy Week, remember? And it's Lent besides. Well, Harry's a renegade Presbyterian, but I'm a dues-paying Episcopalian, and I've always wanted to be married in an Episcopal church by an Episcopal minister, but you simply don't get married in my church during Holy Week and/or Lent. It's against the canons, or something. So we're hung up."

"Then wait for a week or two, or whenever Lent's over."

Roberta looked dreamy.

"We can't. Harry already has our plane tickets — we're spending the night in a hotel and taking off first thing tomorrow morning."

"The solution seems to me not too snarly," Ellery said. "You could cancel the plane tickets."

"We can't," said Roberta. "Harry won't."

"Or you could fly to England tomorrow morning and put the bloody thing off until after Lent."

"It's not a bloody thing, and I wouldn't be able to hold out until after Lent," the Scot said dangerously. "You know, Queen? I don't care for your attitude."

"Ellery," Ellery lamented. "Let's keep this emotional conversation friendly. By the way, how sure are you both that you want to marry each other?"

They stared at him as if he had uttered an indecency.

Then Burke jumped up. "On your feet, Bertie! We're getting the hell out of here."

"Oh, Harry, sit down," Roberta said. He did so reluctantly, eyes spitting colorless murder across the table. "We're sure, Ellery," she said softly.

"You love this character?"

"I love this character."

Ellery shrugged. "Or you could rustle up a minister of some less canonical church to do the job. Or, easiest of all, find some civil servant who's authorized by the State to perform the tribal rites. They're just as binding and a lot less gluey."

"You don't understand," Roberta began; but Inspector Queen came in then with a hogback platter of scrambled eggs, bacon, and buttered toast, and her attention was diverted.

"And I know just the man," the Inspector said, setting the plate down. "The coffee's perking." He explored the sideboard for napkins, plates, and cutlery, and began passing them around. "J.J."

"The Judge," Ellery said damply.

"The Judge?" Burke asked in a suspicious tone. "Who's the Judge?"

"Judge J. J. McCue, an old friend of ours," the Inspector said, and went for the coffee pot.

"Would he do it?" the Scot demanded.

"If dad asks him."

"He's not a minister," Roberta said doubtfully.

"You can't have your eggs and eat them, too, Bertie," her swain said *con amore*. His good humor was on the rise again. "A judge sounds bloody fine to me. Especially the friend-of-the-family type. We can always be married over again by an Anglican priest after we get to England. I don't care how many times I marry you, or how many blokes perform the ceremony, or where. Can you people get Judge McCue today?"

"We can try," the Inspector said, back with the pot. He poured a cupful for Roberta. "If he's

261

in town I'll guarantee it."

Roberta frowned. Finally she nodded, sighed, and said, "Oh, well, all right," and buried her nose in the fragrant cup.

Burke beamed.

Roberta attacked the eggs.

The Inspector sat down and reached for a slice of toast.

But Ellery munched. Tastelessly.

FORTY-TWO

He was in a peculiar humor all day. He did not even perk up at his father's success in locating Judge McCue on a crowded municipal Palm Sunday golf course. So that Harry Burke's dander began to act up again.

"We'll have the ceremony here," the Inspector said, hanging up. "The Judge says he can't do it at his house — his wife comes from a long line of High Church ministers and she thinks Holy Week marriages are made in hell. Besides, he's in enough trouble with her because he's playing golf today. So he'll slip over to our place this evening. Is that all right with you two?"

"Oh, wonderful!" Roberta said, clapping her hands.

"I'm not so bowled over by it," Burke said, glaring at Ellery. "Although it's kind of *you*, Inspector."

Ellery was examining his thumb, which he had just taken out of his mouth. It looked as if a rat had been gnawing at it.

"Harry, my love," Roberta said rapidly. "Don't you have anything to do?"

"Do I?"

"You don't know *anything*."

263

"I've never been married before," her swain said, flushing. "What have I forgotten?"

"Oh, nothing. Just the flowers. My corsage. The champagne. Little things like that."

"My God! Excuse me."

"Don't bother about the bubbly," Inspector Queen called after him. "Ellery has a few bottles of the stuff stashed away for an occasion — haven't you, son?"

"The Sazarac '47? I suppose I have," Ellery said gloomily.

"I wouldn't take his bubbly for all the bubbles in 'em," the Scot said coldly.

"You'll have to," Ellery said, gnawing again. "Where are you going to buy champagne in New York on Palm Sunday?"

Burke stalked out.

"And cigarets, love!" Roberta called. "I'm fresh out."

The door banged.

"I don't know what's come over you two," she said, "— thank you, Ellery," and puffed energetically. "It's not all Harry's fault, either. There's something on your mind. May I ask what it is? Since it's my wedding, and I don't want it spoiled."

"I have problems," Ellery conceded. The Inspector finished his second cup of coffee and glanced at him. "Well!" Ellery rose. "I'd better get the dishes out of the way."

"Here, I'll do them," Roberta said, jumping up. "I don't approve of men doing dishes, even bachelors. You haven't answered my question, Ellery. What problems?"

But Ellery shook his head.

"Why spoil your wedding day? You just said you didn't want it spoiled."

"I certainly do not! I take it all back. You can keep your old problems to yourself."

"Yes," Ellery said; and he disappeared in his study, leaving Roberta frowning a little and his father staring after him thoughtfully.

"What's the matter with that son of yours, Inspector?" Roberta demanded, collecting the plates.

The Inspector was still staring at the door.

"He's in a bind over the Guild case," the old man said. "He always acts this way when a case is bugging him." He followed her into the kitchen, carrying the coffee pot. "Don't let it upset you." He pulled out the tray of the dishwasher for her. "You know, Roberta," the Inspector said suddenly, "it's given me an idea. I wonder if you'd mind."

"Mind?"

"Having a few people in for the ceremony."

Roberta stiffened. "That would depend on who they are."

"Well, Lorette Spanier, Selma Pilter, maybe Mr. Wasser, if we can get them." His tone suggested that the subjunctive mood was a mere courtesy.

"Oh, dear," Roberta said. "Why, Inspector?"

"I don't know why exactly," the old man said.

265

"Call it a hunch. I've seen this sort of thing work with Ellery before. Gathering people who've been involved in a tough case at a critical stage seems to do something for him. Clears his head."

"But it's my wedding!" Roberta cried. "Goodness, people getting married shouldn't be asked to be guinea pigs in a — a —"

"I know it's asking a lot," he said gently.

"Besides, Inspector, Lorette wouldn't come. You know the circumstances under which we broke up. And she's in that revue —"

"Since when are performances of Broadway shows given on Sundays? Anyway, I have a feeling she would. Maybe Lorette's been looking for a chance to make up with you, now that she's hit the jackpot and can afford to let bygones be bygones. And I know you'll feel better about flying off to England without leaving any bitterness behind." Inspector Queen had an old-fashioned belief in the efficacy of "Hearts and Flowers" in situations like these. "What do you say?" he said as he followed her back to the living room.

Roberta silently began to gather up the cups and saucers.

"Be a sport, Roberta."

"Harry wouldn't . . ."

"Leave Harry to me. He's a pro. He understands these things."

"But it's his wedding, too!"

"Think about it. I'd really appreciate it."

266

The Inspector left her quietly and went into Ellery's study. He slipped the door to the living room shut. Ellery was sprawled behind his desk, swivel chair slued about so that he could park his feet on the windowsill and look out at the smog-smutched sky beyond the bars of the fire escape.

"Son."

Ellery kept looking out.

"How about telling me what this is all about?"

Ellery shook his head.

"Are you in the stew, or is it done and you're parked on the lid?"

Ellery did not reply.

"All right," his father said. "I've got to go down to Isaac Rubin's Delicatessen and order some smoked turkey and corned beef sandwiches and stuff for tonight. While I'm out I'd like to phone Lorette Spanier, Carlos Armando, and a couple of others — Mrs. Pilter, William Wasser. Inviting them to the wedding."

That brought Ellery's shoes to the floor in a small explosion.

"That's what you'd be doing if you saw your way clear, isn't it?"

"You know me so damned well it's illegal," Ellery said slowly. "Yes, dad, I suppose it is. But dragging a murder case into a wedding. Do you suppose I'm getting sentimental in my old age? Anyway, you can't very well do it without consulting Roberta and Harry."

"I've already talked to Roberta, although I

didn't happen to mention asking Armando; and I'll handle Mr. Burke. The point is, do you want me to do it?"

Ellery tugged at his nose, cracked a knuckle, and generally agonized.

Finally he said, "Want? Anything but. But I don't suppose I really have a choice."

"Shall I call anyone besides the ones I mentioned?"

Ellery considered. "No," he said, and turned again to the Manhattan sky, which scowled back, puzzled.

He didn't even ask me to get pastrami, the Inspector thought as he slipped out.

FORTY-THREE

Inspector Queen had remarkably little trouble with Harry Burke.

"This wedding is turning out a bugger," the Scot growled to the old man with a shake of his sandy head. "The important thing now is to marry Bertie and get the hell out of your bleeding country, Inspector. By tomorrow morning this will all be a bad dream, I keep telling myself. And Bert and I can wake up."

"That's the boy," the Inspector said warmly, and turned to Roberta, who kicked the rug and said, "Well, if it's all right with Harry."

"That's the girl!"

The old man left for the delicatessen and the outside telephone still without having mentioned Armando. With the Inspector first things came first, and the hindmost could be taken care of by the usual agency.

He had almost as much trouble working his will with Lorette as being waited on by Mr. Rubin, who was puffing about the little delicatessen trying to satiate the demands of the non-Lent-observing Gentiles of his clientele, to whom Isaac Rubin's was an oasis in the Sunday desert. But finally the Inspector succeeded in placing his order, and shut himself up in the telephone booth with some dimes, and girded his lean loins for the fray.

William Maloney Wasser was no problem; the Inspector's argument was Wasser's watchdog responsibility to the famous estate in his care, as if that had anything to do with anything; the lawyer hemmed a little and hawed a little and finally said he supposed he would have to come, even though Roberta West and Harry Burke had nothing to do with anything and he would have to give up *Bonanza* and *Open End*, and what was going on, anyway? With Selma Pilter the Inspector had even less trouble. Her medieval beak sniffed something, too. "Whither Lorette goeth I go, Inspector Queen. I warn you to handle her with kid gloves, she's the hottest property in town. I won't have her so much as bruised. Who did you say are getting married?" The old man neglected to mention that he had not yet invited Lorette, or that Carlos Armando would be there hooked or crooked.

Lorette was difficult. "I *don't* understand, Inspector. Why in the world should Roberta want me at her wedding?"

"Her best friend?" the Inspector said, registering surprise. "Why not, Miss Spanier?"

"Because she's *not* my best friend, or I hers. That's all over with. Besides, if Roberta wants me, why doesn't she invite me herself?"

"Last-minute preparations. They made their plans all of a sudden —"

270

"Well, thank you very much, Inspector Queen, but no thank you."

At this point the Inspector heard a mellifluous *"Cara"* from the background, and Armando's greased murmur.

"Just a moment, please," Lorette said.

An off-telephone discussion followed. The old man grinned in the booth, waiting. Armando was advising acceptance, as of a lark. So he was still riding high, secure in his immunity. So much the better. Ellery should be pleased. And the Inspector wondered for the umpteenth time what Ellery had in mind. And tried not to think of the dirty trick he was playing on the newly-weds-to-be.

"Inspector Queen," Lorette said.

"Yes?"

"Very well, we'll come."

"We?" the old man repeated with cunning bleakness. Two birds with one stone. He had not envisioned Armando as an ally.

"Carlos and I. I won't come without Carlos."

"Well, now, I don't know, Miss Spanier. In view of how Roberta feels about him, not to mention Harry Burke —"

"I'm sorry. If they really want me, they'll have to take Mr. Armando, too."

"All right," the Inspector said, with a not altogether contrived sigh. "I just hope he, uh, respects the solemnity of the occasion. I wouldn't have Roberta's and Harry's wedding spoiled for anything." And hung up, feeling like Judas, a

271

feeling he chased to cover the moment it showed its accusing head.

It's going to be one hell of a wedding, the old man guiltily thought as he left the booth, and for the umpteenth-and-first time wondered what it was all about.

FORTY-FOUR

One hell of a wedding it turned out.

Judge McCue arrived at seven, a tall old party with a white thatch, a bricklayer's complexion, a nose like a prize fighter's, and blue judge-eyes. He towered over Inspector Queen like Mt. Fujiyama. The jurist was glancing at his watch even as the Inspector let him in, and he glanced at it again during the introduction of the unhappy couple, both of whom were beginning to exhibit the classic symptoms of premarital jitters.

"I don't like to hurry matters," Judge McCue said in his Chaliapin voice, "but the fact is I had to tell Mrs. McCue a white lie about where I was going, and she's expecting me back home practically at once. My wife doesn't hold with Lenten weddings."

"I'm beginning to agree with her," Harry Burke said with ungroomlike asperity. "It seems we have to wait, Judge McCue. Inspector Queen's invited some guests to our wedding." The Scot's stress on the pronoun was positively prosecutional.

"It'll be over soon, darling," Roberta said nervously. "Judge, I wonder . . . could you possibly perform the ceremony with the Episcopal

273

service instead of just a civil service? I mean, I'd really feel more married if . . ."

"I don't see why not, Miss West," Judge McCue said. "Except that I don't carry a Book of Common Prayer around with me."

"Ellery's got one in his reference library," Burke said with an anything-to-get-this-over-with air.

"I'll get it," Ellery said unexpectedly. He sounded almost grateful. He emerged from his study with a battered little red-covered book, carrying it as if it put a strain on his arm muscles. "Page 300, I think."

"Don't you feel well, Ellery?" asked Judge McCue.

"I'm fine," Ellery said bravely, and handed the book to the Judge and went over to the windows, between which the enormous basket-spray of shaggy 'mums Burke had ordered had been set up by Roberta for appropriate background, and gloomed down at the street. He kept pulling at his lower lip and pinching his nose, and he looked about as festive as Walter Cronkite announcing an abort at Cape Kennedy.

Burke sniffed the cinnamony air in Ellery's direction, and muttered something.

"Here comes Wasser," Ellery said suddenly. "And Mrs. Pilter."

"Anyone else coming?" Judge McCue referred to his wristwatch again.

"And there's another cab with Lorette," Ellery announced, still looking out, and paused. "And

Carlos Armando," he said.

"What?" Harry Burke shouted in 100-proof stupefaction.

"Now look, Harry boy," the Inspector said hurriedly. "Lorette Spanier wouldn't come without him. I couldn't help myself. If you wanted Lorette —"

"I didn't want Lorette! I didn't want any of them!" the Scot howled. "Whose wedding is this? What's coming off here? By God, for a plugged pig's bladder I'd call the bloody thing off!"

"Harry," moaned Roberta.

"I don't care a tweak, Bertie! These people have taken over the most sacred thing in our lives and they're turning it into a bloody peep show! I won't be used! I won't have you being used!"

"What is this all about?" Judge McCue asked feebly. Nobody answered him.

The door buzzed.

Roberta, half hysterical, raced to the Inspector's bathroom.

The next few minutes were avant-garde and Nouvelle Vague, with a dash of Fellini. The unwilling guests inched in together, to be met by Harry Burke's glare, Ellery's simper, the Inspector's frantic heartiness, and Judge McCue's bewilderment. The only one who seemed to enjoy the experience was Carlos Armando, whose dark face and black eyes glistened with malice. Everyone milled about in the smallish living room,

275

passing and repassing like a deck of cards being shuffled by a clumsy dealer, to the accompaniment of confused introductions, mumbled politenesses, unresponsive grunts, hostile handshakes, enthusiastic references to the dismal spring, sudden silences, overhearty congratulations to Lorette and — like a Wagnerian leitmotiv — queries about the whereabouts of the missing bride, chiefly by Armando, in an innocent tone of voice.

She was in the bathroom "fixing herself up" for the happy event, Inspector Queen found himself saying for the dozenth time.

Ultimately Roberta made her appearance, pale but head high, like the heroine in a Victorian play. The hush that fell over the living room did not improve the climate. Armando's charm poisoned the air; Ellery had to grab hold of Harry Burke's arm at one point to prevent that oak-muscled member from an extremity. In the end it was — suprisingly — Lorette who saved the day. She put her arms about Roberta, kissed her, and took her off to the kitchen to disinter the wedding bouquet from the refrigerator; and when they emerged Roberta announced that Lorette was to be her maid of honor; and the Inspector hastily swiped some 'mums from the basket and improvised a maid of honor's corsage, using a length of white satin ribbon out of the supply he hoarded from past Christmases.

Finally everything was settled. The Judge took up a position between the windows, his back to the floral spray, with Burke facing him on the right hand and Roberta on the left, as prescribed in the liturgy, Lorette standing behind Roberta, Ellery behind Burke, and the others behind them. Judge McCue opened the Book of Common Prayer to page 300, and clamped tortoise shells on his mashed nose, and began in his *basso profundo* to read the Solemnization of Matrimony as ratified by the Protestant Episcopal Church in the United States of America in convention assembled on the sixteenth day of October in the Year of our Lord One Thousand Seven Hundred and Eighty-nine:

"Dearly beloved," the Judge said, and cleared his throat.

Inspector Queen, from his premeditated vantage point to one side, kept watching Ellery. That child of his youth was a stricken man. The Inspector had never seen him so iron-stiff, so bloodless with indecision. Obviously, a worm was nibbling away at the fruit of the Inspector's loins; and, while the Judge read on, the old man kept probing for it, trying to catch and classify. But fruitlessly.

". . . we are gathered together here in the sight of God, and in the face of this company, to join together this Man and this Woman in holy Matrimony . . ."

The room was filled with the odor of the unknown given off by all wedding ceremonies, an odor that is almost a threat. Roberta was unconsciously clutching to her white lace wedding frock the pink velvet muff Burke had ordered,

277

bruising the gardenias with which it was covered; the stocky groom himself seemed inches taller, as if he had suddenly been assigned to sentry duty at Buckingham Palace — the Inspector could almost see Burke wearing a shako and shouldering a musket. Lorette Spanier looked far away and lost. Selma Pilter was secretive with the hidden envy of an old woman to whom weddings were celebrations of regret; and the Inspector was fascinated to behold William Maloney Wasser's belly doing a portly jiggle in rhythm with Judge McCue's cadences, as at some overseen fertility rite. Only Armando was his mocking, hateful self, his enjoyment of the scene evidently deepened by his own multiple experience of such obscenities.

". . . *which is an honourable estate, instituted of God . . .*" The Judge boomed on of the mystical union and the holy estate and the first miracle wrought in Cana of Galilee, and Inspector Queen returned to his only begotten son, stiff as mortality.

And the old man began to wonder with great uneasiness if he had not committed a wrong in taking matters into his own hands. Something wrong, something very wrong, was in the air.

"*. . . and therefore is not by any to be entered into unadvisedly or lightly; but reverently, discreetly, advisedly, soberly, and in the fear of God.*"

Why? Why?

"*Into this holy estate these two persons present come now to be joined.*"

278

What's he wrestling with? the old man thought. Whatever the opponent, the struggle was fierce. A muscle in Ellery's jaw was doing a throttled dance of its own; the hands clasped before him were gray in the knuckles; he stood as rigidly at attention as the nervous groom before him. But Burke has cause, the Inspector thought. What's with my son?

"If any man can show just cause, why they may not lawfully be joined together," the bass voice continued, *"let him now speak, or else hereafter for ever hold his peace."*

Something has to give, the old man's thoughts ran. This can't go on; he'll burst . . . Ellery opened his mouth. And clamped it shut again.

"I require and charge you both, as ye will answer at the dreadful day of judgment when the secrets of all hearts shall be disclosed, that if either of you know any impediment, why ye may not be lawfully joined together in Matrimony ye do now confess —"

Ellery said, "I have a point."

The words sounded involuntary, as if a thought had found its own vehicle of expression, independent of its thinker. And, indeed, Ellery looked as shocked by what he had said as Judge McCue, Roberta West, and Harry Burke. The Judge's severe blue eyes accused him over Burke's head; the nuptial pair half turned in Ellery's direction in protest; and all the other eyes went to him, even Carlos Armando's as if he had given vent to a natural indiscretion during silent prayer in church.

"I have a point," Ellery said again. "I have a point, and I can't keep it to myself any longer. Judge, you will simply have to stop this wedding."

"You're daft," Burke said. "Daft."

"No, Harry," Ellery said. "Sane. Only too sane."

FORTY-FIVE

"I owe you an apology, Roberta," Ellery went on. "This may not seem the time or place, but in another sense it's the only time and place. In either event, I have no choice." He said again, as if to reassure himself, "I have no choice."

He had stepped out of the tableau, while its actors remained frozen where they stood. But now he said, "You had better all sit down, this will take time," as if the concept of time obsessed him; and he moved about, pushing a chair here, settling Roberta with special care, another there, for Mrs. Pilter, and still another for Lorette Spanier. None of the men complied. Already the atmosphere was thickening up to something curiously like a lynching mood. Only, who were the posse and who was the victim?

Ellery braced himself.

"A moment ago I mentioned time and place," Ellery said. "The place may be fortuitous, but what of time? We're face to face with it. Time is of the essence in this case.

"Case . . . Because, of course, the case is what this is all about. The murder case. The murder of Glory Guild.

"I have to take you back to Glory's will, her

281

copy of it," Ellery said, "and what she wrote in disappearing ink between those typewritten lines. What she wrote was an earwitness report of the events of that evening when she overheard her own murder being planned — by you, Armando, when you thought your wife was safely in Connecticut at her cottage, and you got Roberta West up to your wife's apartment and tried to talk this girl into killing her for you."

"You will not take me in by cheap trickery," Armando said, showing his brilliant teeth. "This has all been ably stage-managed, Mr. Queen, but I do not blurt out indiscretions under a surprise. A report in GeeGee's copy of her will? In disappearing ink? You are romancing, no doubt for my benefit. You will have to do better than that."

"The question," Ellery said, turning his back on the swarthy man, "the question is the *time* the incident of the plotting took place. It's the nicest sort of question —"

But he was interrupted. "I can't imagine your doing anything more to me than you're doing at this moment," Harry Burke snarled. "Something's gone wrong with you, Queen. Your brain's begun rattling about in your bean. I don't know what you're talking about."

"The time," Ellery repeated. He took the blue-backed document from his pocket. "This is Glory's copy of her will, with her message on it. You, Harry, and Roberta and Mr. Wasser were present when my father read it aloud in Mr.

282

Wasser's office, so you're acquainted with its contents. The Judge, Lorette, Mrs. Pilter and Armando — especially Armando — are not. So bear with me while I read it to them."

"You probably wrote it yourself," Armando said, smiling; but there was wanness in his smile. "But read it, by all means."

Ellery ignored him. " 'I am writing this for reasons that will become clear soon enough,' " he read. " 'I had wanted for some time to get away from things, and I had planned to go up to Newtown, to the cottage. . . .' " He read on in a neutral, almost schoolmaster's voice, as if it were a lesson to be taught: how Armando's wife had driven up to Newtown and found that her secretary had forgotten her instructions to notify the Connecticut Light & Power Company to turn the electricity on, how the house had been "very damp and cold," and how, rather than risk a cold, she had returned to the city. How she had let herself into the apartment and overheard her husband's conversation with a girl unknown to her; her description of Roberta; Armando's reference to herself as "a cow to be milked"; his proposal to Roberta that she kill his wife while he established an alibi, after which he would inherit "all my money" and marry Roberta. And how, unable to "take any more," Glory Guild had fled from the apartment, walked the streets most of the night, and then driven back to the Connecticut cottage where she had stayed for "two whole days," thinking over her plight; and so on, to the dismal end.

The silence was puzzled, except for Armando's.

"I deny it all, of course," Armando said. "This is a forgery —"

"You be quiet." Ellery tucked the will away in his pocket. "I return to the question. And I ask you: Did you hear a single word in the account I just read you that specifies the *time* when this unlovely scene took place?" And he shook his head. "The fact remains, Glory's message does not date Armando's session with Roberta."

"But Roberta told us the time!" Harry Burke growled. "The night this scum proposed the murder to her — when she ran out of the Guild apartment frightened and disgusted — was a night in May, Roberta said. So what's all this nonsense about time?"

Harry, Harry, Ellery thought.

"Humor me, Harry," Ellery said, "and let's pursue this nonsense. Glory was murdered on the night of December thirtieth last year. You, I, my father went through her diaries and memoirs, with particular attention to last year, and we found every page in last year's diary, up to the day of her death, every page but one jammed with day-to-day jottings. Yet not one of those entries — which means throughout May as well as in any other month last year — not one mentioned what took place in the Guild apartment the night Armando made his charming proposal to Roberta. Not one, or certainly one or all of us — trying to solve the murder — would have

284

pounced on it and shouted it to the rooftops of Centre Street. Nowhere in last year's diary did Glory note down a word about having overheard her husband's plot. That is, directly."

"What do you mean?" Inspector Queen said, frowning. "She didn't mention it at all. You just said so."

"I said 'directly.' But didn't she mention it — as it were — somewhere in the diary indirectly?"

After a moment his father said quickly, "The blank page."

"The blank page. Which was dated what?"

"December first."

Ellery nodded.

"So, in view of its absence everywhere else in the diary, it must have been on the night of December first that Glory overheard Armando plotting her death. And there's a confirmation of this — that blank December first page contained the letters *f-a-c-e* in disappearing ink, which was Glory's read-between-the-lines clue to her copy of the will. Which, duly read, in turn revealed her firsthand account of the events of that night. December first was the date of that session, beyond a doubt.

"December first," Ellery said, addressing himself for the first time in the supercharged silence to Roberta, "not a night in May, Roberta. What's more, there can be no question of its having been a slip of the tongue. You misdated the talk as taking place in May not once but at least twice that I can remember. The first time was on

285

the morning of New Year's Day, when Harry and I had just got off the plane from England — less than thirty-six hours after the murder — and I found my father's note to call you, and I did, and you insisted on coming right over, and you told us about your affair with Armando terminating in his proposal that you kill his wife. He made that proposal to you, you told us, on a night 'a little more than seven months ago.' Since you were telling us this story on January first, 'a little more than seven months ago' placed the conversation some time back in late May.

"One misdating might have been an innocent error, although an error of over half a year takes great faith in innocence to swallow. But you misdated it a second time, the other day, when I finally interpreted Glory's clue *f-a-c-e*, brought out the hidden message in her will, and my father read her accusation aloud in your presence. You immediately placed the time of the scene in the Guild apartment as 'that night in May,' as Harry just reminded us. That was quick of you, Roberta. Before any of us, you spotted Glory's failure to date the scene in her account, and you made on-the-spot use of it to strengthen your original story to us.

"For in that original story, on New Year's morning, you told Harry and me that you had not laid eyes on Carlos Armando between 'that night in May' and the night of December thirtieth, when you said Armando showed up suddenly at your apartment and established his alibi

286

for the murder of his wife, which was taking place presumably while he was with you.

"We know now that you did see the lover you professed to have come to loathe in May — saw him as recently as the night of December first, in his wife's apartment, the night that his proposal to you to murder her really took place, not six months earlier. Far from having dropped him in May, it's a reasonable assumption that you kept seeing him all through the summer and fall — until, in fact, that night of December first.

"And if you lied to us about that, Roberta, then your whole story becomes suspect. And if your whole story becomes suspect, we can no longer take your word for anything you told us. For example, for the alibi you gave Armando for the night of his wife's murder. And if the alibi you gave Armando for his wife's murder is suspect, then it follows that *you yourself have no alibi* for the night of the murder. Because an alibi works two ways, one of them neatly hidden. It accounts for the person being alibied, and *ipso facto* accounts for the person providing the alibi. That was the really clever part of the plan. It cleared you at the same time that it cleared Armando. It enabled you to come to me soon after the murder and, by alibiing your lover, clear yourself of any suspicion that might arise in the investigation.

"Innocent people don't concoct intricate ways themselves of suspicion.

"All this logical figuration, Roberta," Ellery

said to the sorrel-haired girl, "leads to only one conclusion: You could have been the woman Carlos Armando used as his tool. You could have been his accomplice. You could have been the woman we've been hunting — the woman who shot Glory Guild to death."

She was standing pale as a cast; the gardenia-covered symbol of her wedding was pressed hard against her lacy frock, rupturing the flowers. The Scot at her side looked like a companion piece; Burke seemed to be retreating deeper within himself, as if the plaster were hardening; only his transparent eyes showed a tormented kind of life. As for Armando, he wet his pretty lips in the burned and pitted skin and half parted them, as if about to admonish Roberta West against speaking; but then they clamped shut, evidently preferring silence to the risk of admission implicit in a warning.

Ellery half turned from Roberta and Harry Burke, and it was clear that they had become intolerable to him.

But then he turned back. "You could have been," he said to Roberta. "The question is: Were you?

"You were.

"I say this baldly because there are three confirmations of your guilt arising from the facts.

"One: In the account Glory left us between the lines of her will, she described you unmistakably, Roberta, down to the butterfly birthmark on your cheek, as the woman with whom her husband was plotting her death. Since we can no longer accept your word that you rejected Armando's proposal, the fact remains that you were the woman Glory accused. 'This girl is Carlos's accomplice,' she concluded her account. 'She is the one who, if I am murdered, will have done the murder for him.' I submit that Glory would hardly have left such an unequivocal accusation, Roberta, had she not had sufficient reason to believe, from what she overheard that night of December first, that you had given clear evidence of falling in with Armando's plan. Had you remained 'stunned' and 'horrified,' as you told us, 'unable to get a word out,' Glory could not have accused you so without qualification. It follows that you must have said something that night, given some positive indication to Armando, that convinced Glory of your acquiescence in the murder plot.

"And incidentally, let's get one thing straight about the cryptic clue that culminated in the secret account on the will. When Glory sat at her desk on the night of December thirtieth, mortally shot, and managed to pick up a pen and write *f-a-c-e* on a piece of paper before she fell forward on it, it was not an inspiration that came to her from on high a mere few seconds away from death. Now we know that she had prepared that very clue almost a full month earlier, when she wrote the same four letters of the alphabet in disappearing ink on the blank December first page of her diary.

"Also incidentally, Glory's passion for puzzles was not the reason for her use of the *f-a-c-e* clue and the disappearing ink. They were only the *modus operandi* of her motivation. Had she left open instructions and an open account of what she had overheard on December first, she was afraid either Armando or Jeanne Temple, her secretary, who had access to her effects, would find and destroy them — Armando for obvious reasons, Jeanne Temple because she was having an affair with Armando and was presumably under his thumb.

"Which brings us to confirmation number two." Ellery unexpectedly turned to Carlos Armando, who took an involuntary half step backward. "When you planned the murder of your wife, Armando, you believed your premarital agreement with her — that five years' probation business — was no longer in existence; as you said heatedly at the will reading, Glory tore it up before your eyes at the expiration of the five years. Only it turned out that she hadn't done anything of the sort; she had torn up a dummy. So, when Mr. Wasser read the will to the heirs after your wife's funeral, you learned for the first time that she had duped you; that the premarital agreement was still in effect; that all the trouble you had gone to, up to and including masterminding a murder, had netted you a mere $5,000.

"To most murderers this would have been checkmate. A lesser mortal would have given up, collected his $5,000 and turned to other games.

But you were made of more heroic stuff. You didn't give up — not you. You thought you saw a way to recoup your defeat in spite of Glory's defensive play. It's common knowledge that a murderer can't legally profit from his crime. If Lorette Spanier, who inherited the bulk of Glory's estate, could somehow be tagged for her aunt's murder, *the estate would have to revert to you* in spite of that premarital agreement. The reason is, of course, that with Loretta legally out of the picture you would be *the only one* left to inherit. Glory Guild had no other living heirs.

"So you extended your original plan: you framed Lorette for Glory's murder. You knew that a powerful motive could be ascribed to her — the new will naming her the principal heir; that Lorette's denying Glory had told her about the new will had no evidence to back it up. You also knew that Lorette could be charged with opportunity — the then known facts indicated only her unsupported word that she had left her aunt alive in the apartment on the murder night. With motive and opportunity there for the grasping, all you had to do, Armando, was provide Lorette with the third factor of the classical rule: means. You merely had to arrange for the gun that had shot your wife to be found in her niece's possession.

"And who could most easily have planted the gun in Lorette's bedroom closet? You were no longer living in the Guild apartment; but Lorette was, *and Roberta was,* too. So it must have been Roberta who hid the gun in Lorette's hatbox in Lorette's clothes closet. And we know it was Roberta who, when the gun fell out of the hatbox, suggested that Harry Burke and I, in the apartment at the time, be immediately informed of it.

"Third confirmation," Ellery said; and he moistened the dryness in his throat and hurried on, as if anxious to rid himself of an unwelcome burden. "A complication arose. A Bowery derelict called Spotty suddenly appeared, claiming to have information that might clear Lorette of the murder charge. You had already engineered your wife's death, Armando; you had already committed yourself to the frameup of Lorette; you wanted Glory's estate more than ever; the only thing to do, you reasoned, was to get rid of Spotty before he could testify and clear Lorette, destroying your last chance to get your hands on all that loot.

"So, Armando, you did just that. You got rid of Spotty. Since he was killed in that Bowery flophouse, you must have got in there dressed as a bum, registered under a false name, gone up to the 'dorm,' stabbed Spotty as he lay on the cot, and either walked out calmly into the winter night under Burke's nose or escaped through the rear exit.

"But the question is, how did you even know of Spotty's existence, Armando? How did you become aware of the danger he posed to your

292

frame-up of Lorette? Most important of all, how did you learn where to find Spotty? You were not in Uri Frankell's office when Spotty showed up offering to sell his information. Ah, *but Roberta was.* And, what's more, she accompanied Harry Burke when he immediately set about trailing Spotty from Frankell's office to the Bowery. So it's evident that when Roberta left Burke on watch outside the flophouse for a few minutes and went off to that cafeteria to buy some sandwiches, she took the opportunity to phone you, Armando. It's the only way you could have found out so quickly about Spotty's unexpected appearance as a vital factor in the case, and why, when, and where to kill him.

"So there it is," Ellery said wearily "the whole dreary *shtik,* act and scene and line. It was a magnificently clever plot, if you go into ecstasies over this sort of thing — brilliantly worked out, brilliantly executed, brilliantly improvised when improvisation was called for, and as sickening an exercise in misdirected ingenuity as I've run across in some years.

"Roberta, you were the one who got into the Guild apartment that night of December thirtieth with a duplicate key Armando provided; you were the one who insinuated yourself into the case so as to be on the inside, a reliable source of information to Armando as it arose in the course of the official investigation. By the way, you must originally have intended to shine up to me, as close to the police officer in charge; but when

Harry Burke fell for you, you decided it would be safer and subtler to switch your attentions to him, knowing he would have as much access to the inquiry as I had. And you were the one, Roberta, who put us on the trail of a woman who didn't exist — the 'other' woman you led us to believe Armando must have used as his tool in the killing, when it was you all along. And you were the mysterious woman in the violet veil who, once the murder was done, was significantly never seen again. You were not only the murderer in this case, Roberta, you also acted as its prime red herring — a combination rare in the hankypank of murder."

There was an inexorability in the progress of Ellery's tired voice, an end-of-the-road quality, that was more frightening than a riot squad. Roberta stood immobilized by it. As for Armando, his black eyes were fixed on her with extraordinary violence, straining to communicate warnings, threats, reminders. But it was as if she did not see him, or anyone.

"I'm almost finished," Ellery said, "and if I leave anything out, or get anything wrong, Roberta, you can supply the omission or correct the error." (*No!* screamed Armando's black eyes.) "I imagine that the crisis in your relationship with Armando occurred with the failure of the frame-up against Lorette — with her acquittal at the trial. From that moment your interests diverged. Glory Guild's fortune, or the share you were working toward, Roberta, was irretrievably out of your reach.

"But was it out of Armando's reach? Hardly. Armando has the instincts of a vampire bat. He got busy charming Lorette as he had charmed so many women before her, including her aunt; and you realized, Roberta, that now he meant to marry her and so get his hands on the fortune he had failed to grasp through murder. If and when that happened, there was no place in the game for you. You were of no further use to Armando except for your mutual alibis, and that was a Mexican standoff. Being a woman, you overreacted. You began to warn Lorette against Armando, trying to thwart his new plan . . . trying, I suppose, to salvage the only thing left to you out of the whole sorry business, Armando himself. You must have been wildly in love with him in the first place to let him talk you into committing murder for him; and now that you saw yourself losing him to Lorette . . ."

"And what about me?" Harry Burke demanded in a cawing croak, like a jungle bird.

"What about you, Harry?" Ellery said deliberately, but he did not sound as if he were enjoying himself. "Do you still dream the fairy-tale dream that Roberta is in love with you? You were a pawn in this game, Harry, a very minor piece to be sacrificed on the board."

"Then why is she marrying me? Why," the Scot wheeled on Roberta for the first time, "are you marrying me?"

Roberta moistened her lips. "Harry . . ."

295

"What de'il's use can I have for you as a husband?"

"Harry, I did fall in love with you. I do love you."

"With your hands stained with blood!"

Her lips quivered, and when she spoke it was in so low a voice that they all had to strain to hear her. "Yes . . ." But then it gathered strength. "Yes, Ellery's right about everything — the murder, everything — I did shoot her —" (*No, no, no!* shrieked Armando's eyes.) "— but not about that. I've been trying to forget the whole nightmare. I wanted to start a new life . . ."

"Idiot!" shouted Carlos Armando. "Stupid, stupid idiot! And now you have fallen into Queen's trap. All he wanted out of you was an admission of guilt, and you have given it to him. Don't you realize even in your stupidity that if you had kept your mouth shut they could have done nothing against us? In all Queen's fancy talk, they have not a particle of evidence they could take into a courtroom! *Fool. FOOL!*"

Inspector Queen said, "Miss West, are you willing to make a sworn statement?"

Roberta looked at Harry Burke. What she saw in his face made her turn away. "Yes," she said to the Inspector. "Yes."

FORTY-SIX

The jets were coming and going; the planned chaos of the airport swirled and swooped and buzzed around them unseen and unheard. They might have been in a cave on an island in a typhoon as they waited for Burke's flight to be announced.

The Scot's eyes were no longer transparent; they were the color of blood. He looked as if he had not slept or changed his clothes for a week. His mouth was zippered. He had not asked Ellery to see him off; he had made it plain, in fact, that he wanted never to see Ellery again. But Ellery had tagged along undiscouragedly.

"I know how you feel, Harry," Ellery was saying. "I used you, yes. I almost didn't. I fought with myself not to. When Lorette sang Jimmy Walker's song and that December-May business hit me between the eyes and I saw the whole thing clear, I fought the toughest fight of my life. I didn't know what to do, how to handle it. And when you and Roberta came over and announced you meant to be married right away — last night — the fight was even tougher. Because it gave me an opening, a way to get her to confess. And then my father proposed inviting the

297

others to the wedding. He knows me through and through; he knew something final was in the wind, and without knowing my destination he knew what to do to get me off the ground.

"In the end I gave in, Harry. I had to; I suppose there was never any real doubt about what I had to do. I had no choice. Armando was right: nothing in my argument about Roberta's guilt could have constituted a court case. So I had to make Roberta confess. And not only that. I also had to find a way to stop you from marrying her. I couldn't let you marry a murderess, and I knew that only an admission from her lips would convince you that she was just that. And, of course, I couldn't let a murderess go scot-free . . . no, that's a foul pun; I didn't intend it."

"British Overseas Airways flight number nineteen now loading at Gate Ten," said the annunciator.

Burke grabbed his flight bag and began to stride toward Gate Ten, almost running.

Ellery hurried after him.

"Harry."

The Scot turned on him then. He said in a murderous voice, "You go to hell," and muscled his way through the crowded gate, shouldering an old lady aside, so that she staggered and almost fell.

Ellery caught her. "He's not feeling well," he explained to the old lady.

He stood there until long after Gate Ten was empty. While the BOAC jet taxied to its runway.

Until it was part of the sky, and lost.

Of course Burke was being unfair. But you couldn't expect a man to be fair when he had just had his whole life kicked out from under him.

Or the man who had done the kicking to soothe himself with the perfect music of reason.

And so Ellery stood there.

He was still standing alone on his island when a hand touched his.

He turned around and it was, of all people, Inspector Queen.

"El," his father said, squeezing his arm. "Come on, I'll buy you a cup of coffee."

A face that had a story to tell. How different faces are in this particular! Some of them speak not. (Some) faces are books in which not a line is written, save perhaps a date.
HENRY WADSWORTH LONGFELLOW

The employees of G.K. Hall hope you have enjoyed this Large Print book. All our Large Print titles are designed for easy reading, and all our books are made to last. Other G.K. Hall books are available at your library, through selected book-stores, or directly from us.

For information about titles, please call:

(800) 257-5157

To share your comments, please write:

Publisher
G.K. Hall & Co.
P.O. Box 159
Thorndike, ME 04986